Fate
VS
Choice

TJ Lee

A fated mate is the person who was born to be your mate. A person you have never met before but know within minutes that they were always meant to be yours.

A chosen mate is the person you met, got to know, and fell in love with. Someone you choose to spend your life with.

So, which is better? Fate or Choice.

PROLOGUE

No one really knew why or how it started, but every wolf was born with a fated mate somewhere out in the world. A mate that was created just for them. Some believed that a fated mate was part of their soul. Some believed that their fated mate was their perfect match, the one shifter who was exactly what they needed to balance them out. Others believed their fated mate gave them a better chance at continuing the shifter race and keeping their strength.

Unfortunately, as humans spread throughout the world, so did shifters. Populations grew and more packs were needed. It wasn't just the humans that settled into the new parts of the world. Shifters wanted more freedoms as well. Many hoped the new lands would give them more space to run free. To live how they wanted. To be true to who they were. They rushed to get the best pieces of land. They wanted to claim as much as possible for their pack.

As a result, new problems arose for shifters. First, packs began to fight for control over the best lands. Hard feelings rose until packs went to war. The rogue population increased as they were banished (or just left) from their packs.

Second, which was affected by the increase in violence, was that finding their fated mates was harder than ever before. While the human population was on the rise, shifters were not. They saw a decrease in population because so many wolves were waiting for their fated mates. It was tradition. It was expected.

But what if their mate had been born to a pack that had relocated to the new lands?

Of course, it didn't help that they were killing each other either.

A new trend began. The trend of choosing a mate. This wasn't something that was completely new. Although rare, it had been known to happen from time to time in the past. The only blessing was that once a wolf was marked, and marked another, the call of a fated would fade away. It would fade away to the point that they could be standing right next to their fated mate and not even know it. The new trend became popular in some packs. Packs that were further from others and were small. Small enough that every wolf knew each other. There was no missing a fated mate in those packs.

No matter the circumstances, the fear of missing out on your fated was in the mind of every wolf. Should they choose a suitable mate, when their fated could show up any day? If they did choose, wouldn't they always know that there was someone out there that would have been better for them?

Fate vs choice.

What would you pick? Would you wait? Would you scour the world searching? Or would you find a wolf that you could love and choose them to be your mate?

But... what if you chose wrong?

CHAPTER 1

Cassie

"Are you sure you want to do this, Cas? Seattle is so far away. Too far. Who will be there to protect you?"

Ever since my older sister Katie died, Pat had become extra protective of me. That was sixteen years ago. He had always been a protective big brother, it just got worse after.

And it was getting a little old.

We were getting a little old for this.

I sighed quietly, knowing he wasn't trying to be overbearing. Pat was a good brother who only wanted to ensure he didn't lose another sister. I just had to keep reminding myself of that.

Regularly.

"I can protect myself. Besides, dad already spoke to the Alpha of the local pack. I will not be the only wolf new to the area, but I will still mainly be around humans." I kissed one of his cheeks softly and then patted the other one, not so softly. "Pretty sure I can handle them." I added a sassy wink. "I took you down, didn't I?"

He groaned and rolled his eyes. My big brother was three inches taller than me, and had about a hundred pounds on me, but I still took him down in training last week. It was awesome! And even if it never happened again (which it probably wouldn't) I would never let him live it down as long as I lived.

Our pack may be small, but we knew how to fight. We had too. When you lived in the middle of nowhere, with some of the best natural resources in the country, you needed to be able to protect your pack and territory.

"That was a fluke, and you know it." Pat's arms folded across his wide chest, purposely making the muscles in his arms pop out. It made him look like an overgrown, irritated toddler.

I gleefully described, and maybe rubbed it in a little, exactly how that fluke happened.

We had been sparring for ten minutes, and he had already taken me down twice. I circled him, preparing to swipe his legs out from under him. Unfortunately, he always knew when I was about to do that. I wasn't the best fighter in our pack, but I wasn't the worst either. I was getting extremely frustrated with the situation, and if I wasn't careful, he would use that against me.

Behind my back, we heard the sounds of the door to the pack gym open. There weren't any classes going on today, it was open to all ages and levels at this time. So, I ignored it. I had more important things on my mind.

Pat ignored it at first too, but then he sniffed. He took a quick glance before turning back to me. Then he looked again. Curious, I took a few steps to the right, he countered, keeping that distance from me. He had one eye on whoever entered, and one eye on me. I took a few more steps, making it harder for him. Soon, he was having to turn more to see who had come in.

I had a better view by that point, so I looked up, and then grinned. Pat was distracted looking at a certain female. Using the advantage of a good distraction, I swiftly dropped to my left leg and swung my right leg out in front of me. Within seconds, he fell to his back with an oof. Without missing a beat, I jumped back up and put my foot to his neck. And then did a little dance.

That certain female giggled as she passed.

When you were the smaller fighter, you took every opportunity given to you. A real battle was never going to be clean. So, why should I practice clean fighting? I wanted to be prepared for whatever would come.

And take my brother down whenever I could. It was my job, as the younger sister, to bring him down a peg - or a leg - from time to time. Keep that ego of his in check.

The *certain* female, Stacey, was new to our little pack. She and her family moved here just under a year ago. She was old enough that she didn't have to come with them, but wolves were pack animals at heart. Family was really important to us. So, unless they had a mate or a job that couldn't transfer, they followed their families.

Such was not the case for Stacey. She had no mate to speak of when they left Florida, and her degree was in teaching. As she had just finished earning her degree in Education, it was easy to move and find a job. Especially when it was a school close to pack lands. She came in as the new third grade teacher at the local elementary school. The principal was part of our pack.

The population here was about fifty-fifty. Half wolves and half humans. Not that the humans were aware of that of course. They didn't know we existed. Well, not as shifters anyway. Obviously they knew about the small town that was located further into the mountains. And they knew there was a high population of wolves there. They just didn't know the two were one in the same.

Yes, I know. That made it sound like there were a lot of wolves running around these mountains, but there really weren't.

Our pack, The Denali Pack, resides in the Alaska Range. Our territory covers from the Gulf of Alaska (which included all the peninsulas and islands) up to Fort Yukon. Our pack and the Arctic pack split our lovely little state in half. We had the Southern portion, and they had the Northern.

Those lines were drawn many, many years ago. After many, many small wars.

Alaska itself contained less than 800,000 people. Where we lived, in the Range, including Denali, was just over 2,000 inhabitants. Okay, so maybe we weren't quite fifty-fifty with the humans, not completely anyway. The humans preferred to live near the big cities, whereas the wolves preferred the mountain regions.

Anyway, the point in that little geography lesson was to help you understand that we were pretty isolated here. But I probably just ended up confusing you more. Sorry.

Anyway, unless your fated mate was in our pack - the Arctic pack - or the Yukon pack (our Canadian neighbors that were not exactly near us), you probably were not going to find them. My brother wouldn't be the first wolf to settle for a chosen mate.

Sadly, most of us grew up knowing we were mostly going to have to choose our mate. That wasn't necessarily a bad thing though. It was always nice to be in control of your own future. Even if it meant knowing there was someone even better out there for you. The hope was that you chose someone you couldn't imagine being able to top.

Divorce wasn't exactly something shifters could do.

My parents were some of the lucky few, the rare-mated couples that found their fated match. My mom and her roommates were celebrating finishing nursing school when they flew to Anchorage to spend a week of freedom. That's what they called it. They wanted to see real snow. For longer than the ten minutes it would take for it to melt, anyway. The monumental amounts of greenery we had in the Range was a nice pull too.

The Mojave pack, my mom's birth pack, was located in Southern California. Even in Alaska, Mojave was known for its heat. It was home to Death Valley, which was also known for being the hottest, and driest, area in North America.

The four friends were out hiking one day, near Susima River, when one of my mom's friends lost her footing and slipped. The timing was not on her side. It could have been worse though. She only slid a few feet down a small cliff, landing on a ledge, breaking her ankle. That ledge was the last stop before a straight fall into the cavern below. So, she did have some luck that day.

Two of the friends ran down the hill, to where they had a better signal, and called for help. The other, mom, waited on the mountain for search and rescue. As the only shifter, she had no fears about being alone in the forest and mountains. She did her best to try and keep her friend calm, hollering down to her so she wouldn't feel abandoned and alone.

As soon as her friend was safe, mom shifted and ran down the mountain to join the others at the hospital.

My dad was doing his internship at the local hospital at the time. He claimed he could smell my mom the moment she walked through the ER doors.

For a human, that probably wasn't a compliment. I mean, she had just spent the day outside. She was probably feeling pretty sweaty and gross by that point. For a wolf though, it meant something. Something big.

Dad had been professional and mature about it though.

He walked up behind her, spun her around, growled "mine," and kissed her. The shifters in the room laughed. Mom's friends were just plain confused.

Mom had only been inside for about two minutes before he did that. It was good timing on his part though, her wolf needed the comfort after the day they had. They were both worried about their friend.

When the vacation week was up, Mom went home to Mojave long enough to pack her things, tell her family that she had met her fated mate, pack, then flew right back to my dad. The day after she moved to Alaska, she started working in the pack hospital. Once dad finished his internship, he transferred there too.

We visited our desert cousins in California every year, usually during winter or Spring break. No one wanted to go during the summer. It was hot enough during the cooler seasons, we didn't want to experience the summer months.

For the last year, I had been encouraging Pat to go talk to Stacey. Preferably before another male wolf did. She was getting a lot of attention. The new toy, so to speak. My brother was too chicken to do it though. He didn't exactly get out much.

Pat was very dedicated to his studies. He recently finished his internship at the University hospital and was preparing to do his residency at a hospital closer to home. Even though he was obviously very distracted by Stacey - hence me being able to take him down - he wanted to wait until he was more settled to do anything about it. She deserved more than a "part-time mate," as he put it.

For the last two years, he and I shared an apartment near campus together. With him leaving, I was going to be on my own anyway, so I decided to go even further. I chose Seattle University. They had a decent Psychology and pre-med program.

I hadn't decided if I wanted to be a doctor like my dad and brother, or a nurse like my mom. I basically grew up in a doctor's office. The world of medicine and helping people was all I really knew. Not that I was complaining. I liked helping others to feel better. I guess it ran in the family.

I'd always been in awe of how my dad could tape people back together. Or the times where he got to help them figure out what was wrong.

But on the other hand, my mom had the privilege to sit down and get to know the patients better. She spent more time with them. Helping to soothe the scared pups or being that one person that someone could finally feel free to tell all their woes too.

Both were equally awesome, hence my need to figure out what I wanted still.

Moving away might be just what I needed too. I was hoping a new place, with new people, would help me figure out what I wanted, and which path was right for me. I wanted to experience life. I loved my pack, and my town. But there was so much world out there. So many different kinds of people.

While rubbing in exactly how I beat Pat had lightened the mood, my big brother still wasn't happy about our impending separation.

"One way or another, I was still going to be living away from you, Pat. I'm a big girl. I need you to trust me. Please."

He leaned in and gave me another big hug. It was tight enough that I could feel his wolf whimper in his chest. They both were such softies. They were more like a giant teddy bear than a giant wolf.

"I know, Cas. I just worry about you." My brother stepped away from me and picked up my last bag to carry it to the car. "Promise me you aren't going to get distracted with all the parties there. I know you."

"I promise not to get distracted by them, but I won't promise not to go. If anything, I will just study human behavior in a party scene. You know I've always been fascinated by them."

Pat chuckled softly and shook his head at my go-to excuse for some of the more daring (and no doubt stupid) things I'd done.

"Sure, pup. Just be careful, please?"

Mom and dad were waiting near the mini-SUV my mom drove every day, so they could take me to the airport. We all piled in silently and drove together. All three of them wanted to be there to see me go or talk me out of it. It was still a toss-up.

I was putting on a good front, but I was really nervous about leaving them.

At the airport, they followed me through check-in, and all the way up to security. Where I was then given more hugs by my family. The male members had wetter eyes than the females. Big softies.

They didn't care about showing emotions as much as the more dominant wolves in the pack would have. I never confirmed it, they were still males and had egos after all, but I always had the suspicion that my mother and I had more dominant wolves than my dad and brother.

Which could be why she and I were more adventurous. And why Pat was dragging his feet on talking to Stacey.

Don't get me wrong, I love to sit around a fire with a good book. I could even tear up at a sad part in movies or books. But I also liked to go out to meet new people and have fun. I admit, I typically ended up somewhere towards the side of the crowd, not exactly in the middle. I wasn't really a fan of all that attention. Plus, I really did like to observe people when they were going about their daily business. I usually had a better view from the sidelines anyway.

Mom called me her little conundrum. I was neither introverted, nor extroverted. I was right smack dab in the middle of both. It all just depended on my mood.

Mom ended up having to step in and help me with moving my dad away, forcing him to let go of me. His arm still stayed in a side hug as they walked me all the way through the airport. It was like he was afraid I would disappear too soon.

As we walked, mom told us stories about how they used to be able to walk all the way up to the gate with whoever was traveling. Pat and I both blanched as she told us about the farewell between her and my dad at the gate, right after they first met. We gagged when they pretended to reenact it for us.

Mom got a good laugh at that. Dad looked embarrassed, even though he was just as involved as she had been. Not that he would ever deny mom anything.

The stories all said how hard it was to be away from your fated mate. They told us how there was this overwhelming driving need to take care of them, to always be there for them. Fated mates were similar to the human version of soul mates. Or so I have been led to believe.

I liked a good romance novel once in a while. Humans, or shifters, it didn't matter. It wasn't like human authors could get the shifter one right anyway. Their take on us usually cracked me up, seeing as they didn't think we were real and could use creative license. It was always fun to come across ones you just knew were written by shifters. It was like finding that diamond in the rough.

Anyway, as I was saying, fated mates were that one shifter that was made specifically for you. In our pack, there was a myth that when shifters were created, it was done similar to that of Adam and Eve. God took a rib from Adam to create Eve. Well, the myth says that God took a piece of the first Alpha shifter's soul to create his female, his Luna. Your fated mate was said to have that piece of your soul.

I never understood why we had chosen mates if that was the case though. My mother told me that at some point, it became very difficult to find fated mates, because shifters were spreading so far out. It became necessary to settle for chosen mates.

There have been many debates on whether this was wise, seeing as how there was a danger to the family and pack if the fated mate showed up later. It would make it difficult for the mate to stay with their chosen family.

Somehow, it was discovered that mating with a chosen mate erased the bond with the fated one. I always wondered if that meant someone had rejected their fated mate, for whatever reason (I knew of a few that probably should have done that, sweet females, jerky males, go figure) and then mated with a chosen. They must have felt the pull to their fated mate disappear.

As time went on, the chances of finding your fated mate decreased. Especially for the more submissive wolves. The dominant ones, like the Alphas, betas, and such, always found theirs easier. I guess that had something to do with stronger wolf senses or fate trying to keep the bloodlines of our leaders as strong as possible.

Who knew, really? It wasn't like shifters had history books like humans did. That wouldn't be safe. For the most part, we kept hidden from the outside world.

Humans were idiots. They freaked out over the slightest thing. They couldn't even handle people from the same species who looked differently than them. Spoke differently. Believed differently. The slightest difference made them uncomfortable. If they were to find out about us, all hell would break loose.

Well, worse than it already was, I guess. It seemed like they were always finding something to fight over. I mean, wolves could be violent creatures too, but we were generally more accepting than they were.

So, one mate was darker than the other, what was the problem? It just meant their packs were from different climates and their human forms adapted to better protect them. They shifted the same as we did. They found mates the same as we did. They had thoughts and feelings just like everyone else did. It sure as hell didn't mean there was something wrong with them.

Human behaviors often reminded me of that book, *The Giver*. Everyone wore the same basic thing. There was no such thing as diversity. Pretty soon, the people had no freewill. It sounded like a very dull and boring life to me.

If people were all the same color - hair, and skin - where would the diversity be?

If we all believed exactly the same, where would the diversity be?

Life would stagnate.

Life would be *boring!*

We might as well all live in *Pleasantville*, and have everything be black and white, with nothing ever changing.

By the time my mother managed to separate the males from me, again, I could hear my flight being boarded. Thankfully, my gate wasn't far from security. That and I had dressed ready for removing my shoes, and not a stitch of metal on me. Not even a zipper - thank you to whoever invented leggings!

My flight lasted just over three hours, nearly five if you counted all the times we sat on the tarmac. Before and after the flight.

It sucked when people basically ran to catch their flight, just to sit in line to take off. Seriously. Why did that take so long? Didn't they schedule this stuff in advance?

I did get lucky though. The flight was long enough that it had an in-flight movie. Which probably wasn't the best of choices for a plane ride...*2012*. Really, a movie about the end of the world?

It got really dicey in the beginning, when the family was trying to fly away from the earth that was caving underneath them. Seriously?

I wasn't the only person who kept peeking out their window to make sure the earth was still there, especially when we hit turbulence. That was some pretty mind twisting stuff right there.

Let's just hope people weren't stupid enough to watch *Titanic* while on a cruise.

From the Seattle airport, after waiting an eternity for our turn to approach a gate, I ordered an Uber with my phone. I was so excited to use that app for the first time. Not many Uber drivers in the middle of nowhere Alaska.

Not many places you couldn't just shift and run to either. Backpacks were a necessity of life.

Pat wasn't thrilled with the idea of me Ubering to campus. Such a worrywart. He was going to be very happy to hear that my driver was a sweet older lady in her sixties. Young enough to still be allowed to drive (in his mind) but old enough that I got lots of stories about her grandbabies graduating high school in a year.

The very chatty lady dropped me off in front of the campus dorms, where I would be staying for the next year or more.

Who knew what the future might bring?

When we pulled up, I got out of the small Prius slowly, taking in all the people and buildings around me. I giggled with pure joy. I had never been away from home on my own before, or lived with someone who wasn't blood related. I was thrilled.

My driver popped the trunk and helped me pull out my two large duffle bags in addition to the backpack I used as a carry-on. I could only take so much on the plane with me. To help me be comfortable, my parents gave me a debit card, and made me promise to get anything else I needed to furnish my dorm room. I fully planned to go shopping later, hopefully with my new roommate.

I didn't know much, or really anything, about her. All I knew was that she was supposed to be a shifter as well.

It was comforting to know that I wasn't the only shifter there. My Alpha called the local Alpha, something like professional courtesy or whatever. He told my dad and I that the local pack, the Olympic Pack, kept an eye on the campus. I wasn't the only non-pack wolf who would be attending. They even had a wolf who worked in the administration office, in the housing department. By design of course.

They made sure shifters roomed together. I guess going away for school was a common thing to do.

I took a quick picture with my driver, in front of the sign to my dorms, before she left, and sent it to my brother.

Me: Proof I arrived safely and not all Uber drivers are psychotic killers.

I laughed when his response came back before I even made it to the front doors.

Pat: You can't judge people by their looks. She may be a black widow and you would never know.
Pat: Glad you are safe. Love you.

I laughed again as I responded.

Me: *smack my head emoji* love you too. Now go ask Stacey out.

I giggled one last time after stuffing my phone into the side pocket of my backpack. I was going to have the last laugh, one way or another. I could be just as annoying as him.

Carefully, I re-secured the bag to my back. It did contain my laptop after all. No need to break that on day one. Then I lifted a duffle in each hand and headed for the doors leading into my assigned building.

As the emailed instructions had directed, I walked up to a table that said "New Student Information Here." I waited in the semi-long line for ten minutes, until it was my turn. The girl at the table popped a bubble with her gum and gave me that fake smile.

"Name?" Her fake cheerful voice asked.

"Cassandra Goodall."

She looked at the papers on her desk and rummaged through the first pile, the one that had a sticky note labeled A-G on it. With her finger she scrolled down a long list, until she reached the end of the second page. Where she found my name and room number. Then she switched to a large index file and rifled through, pulling out a credit card looking key.

"You are in room 417. Welcome to Seattle U. We are happy to have you." She picked up a blue folder and handed it to me, with my key on top.

I had already set my bags down, tired of holding them up, while I waited. Yes, shifters were stronger than humans. But my flight had been early in the morning, and it had been a very long day so far. This shifter was pooped.

I sighed as I put the folder under my arm, so I could lift my bags again, and kept the key between my fingers for easy access.

"Take the elevator to your left, up to the fourth floor, follow the signs from there. A map and any other information about the dorm and your RA are in that folder. Have a good day."

Before I could even respond, she was looking behind me, yelling "Next!" With more fake cheerfulness. I didn't like to judge people too quickly, but I was fairly certain that she and I were not going to be friends.

Alrighty, then. I took a deep breath, preparing myself, as I trudged along once again.

I walked over to the elevator the not-so-helpful girl pointed out and waited. There were a lot of people roaming about, a good many of them holding luggage like me. A few had parents and siblings with them, helping them carry boxes and bags. I watched one hugging a tearful mother, her eyes pleading with her father for help.

Out of everything, that made me homesick the most. I was already missing my family. I hadn't experienced anything like this before. Pat and I lived in the same dinky apartment for two years, the only time I had lived away from my parents. And it had only been an hour away from home.

I had a few friends that lived in the dorms back home, but I rarely ever went inside with them. We usually met up at restaurants, cafes, or benches in the common areas.

My wolf felt more homesick than I did. I could feel her cuddled into a small ball of fur in the back of head.

Once I reached my floor, it was simple enough to find my dorm room.

I frowned as I passed the restrooms. The door opened as I passed, and I got a sight of the showers.

Lovely.

I wasn't looking forward to sharing a bathroom with more than a dozen other females. Or showering in a stall.

On the bright side, my room was only two doors down from there. At least I wouldn't have far to go if I woke up in the middle of the night and had to pee.

I should probably add new pajamas to my shopping list. For one, it wouldn't be as cold here. For another, mine were a bit holey from years of use. They had been well loved and abused.

CHAPTER 2

Cassie

The door to 417 was closed. I gave an exhausted sigh and tried to unlock my door without putting the bags down. It didn't work. I ended up just dropping a bag and unlocked the door, which was much easier that time.

With that done, I glanced down at my bag, deciding whether I really wanted to pick that sucker back up.

Nope. I did not.

I looked around my assigned room, getting a feel for my new home, all while pushing the door open enough to kick the bag through. It took more energy than I had. Apparently it wasn't just my arms that were worn out.

The room was maybe twice the size of my bedroom back home, but it was meant to hold an extra person as well. Both the left and right sides held a twin-size bed, with two small desks in between them. There were two windows on the wall behind them, one for each bed. The walls next to them were bare, as were the beds and desks.

At the foot of each bed was a narrow door. I opened one of them and discovered it to be a small closet, barely big enough for one person to go inside. There were no dressers, but the closets did have shelves.

Next to the door to the hall was a small kitchenette. Calling it a kitchenette was being generous. It was really just a small counter, with two small cabinets underneath, and a minifridge on the counter. The counter held a sink the size of a small bathroom sink.

In fact, my bathroom counter at home may have been bigger than the kitchen counter here was. Maybe we could at least fit a toaster oven on it. That would be good for bagels in the morning.

The whole room was painted in a light brown color, just a hint darker than cream. The furniture was roughly the same color. It was all bland and boring. Something I was definitely going to have to remedy.

Seeing as it didn't look like my new roomie was there yet, I went ahead and picked the right side of the room. I unpacked my clothes. I hung them up on these weird hangers that looked like they were built into the rod and folded my more private items and put them on the shelf. I was going to have to get a small bin to keep them in. I wasn't comfortable with just having them out like this. If someone walked into my closet, hopefully a new friend helping me pick out an outfit, they would get a front row seat to my unmentionables. No, thank you.

It was called Victoria's Secret for a reason. It was not Victoria Tells All.

Next came the entertainment section of my bags. I had a few books that I packed to bring with me, for when I desperately needed to read something besides textbooks. I set them up on my desk, along with my laptop, alarm clock, and chargers for my phone and said laptop.

And that was it. Less than an hour in my dorm room and I was already unpacked. I sank onto my still naked bed and started contemplating what to do next. Thankfully, I was saved by the door opening.

I sniffed before turning, a habit every shifter held, and smiled to myself. At least I wouldn't have to hide what I was when I was at home. That would be nice. I turned my eyes to the door and saw the female who entered. She looked worn out and somewhat irritated. Just like me!

My new roomie had short, spiky, purple hair. She had piercings covering the entirety of both ears, and what looked like a nose ring. My first thought, I was definitely not in Kansas anymore.

What? I liked *The Wizard of Oz*. Shoot me.

"Hi! I'm Cassie." I stood up to greet her.

She gave me a forced half smile that looked more like a grimace. "Yolanda."

She detoured straight for the other bed and dropped her bags.

I sat back down on the edge of my bed gingerly, pushing back far enough to fold my legs under me.

"Long day?"

Yolanda huffed and plopped down on her bed, harder than her bags had when they hit the floor. "You could say that. I was supposed to be here this morning, but my parents couldn't stop arguing long enough about which way we should take." She rolled over on her side to face me, her hand holding her head up. "It's not like we haven't made this trip before, ya know?" She growled softly again and rolled to her back.

"Where are you from?" I asked carefully, trying to gauge whether she was even up for talking. I didn't want to alienate her from the beginning. I wanted us to start out on the right foot. Set a good foundation.

Okay, so maybe I was a little anxious about how well we would get along.

"Spokane!" Her hand flew up into the air above her. "It's only supposed to be four hours! It was practically a straight shot West!" Her hand fell over her eyes as she let her body shake in a dramatic whimper. "What about you?" She asked after a few deep breaths.

"Denali."

Yolanda seemed to freeze and then started laughing. I waited it out. I had a feeling I knew what was coming next. All newcomers to Denali said something along the same lines.

"Sorry, sorry." She pulled herself up into a sitting position, her feet falling to the floor, facing me once again. "I didn't even realize that was a real place. I only ever heard of it from *Twilight*. Knowing that it's wolves that live there and not vampires...well, it's kind of funny."

I smirked. "You wouldn't be the first. Many of the tourists that come through there ask if we have vamps. If only they knew the truth, right?"

We talked for a few more minutes, covering all the basics while she unpacked. Yolanda was studying to be a Social Worker. She'd been attending Seattle U for three years now. This was her last year, putting her a year ahead of me.

"I don't know about you, but I could use a run. After that, we can swing by a Target and get you some bedding and stuff. I don't have a car, but Uber always works for me."

"Sounds perfect. My wolf is still feeling antsy from the flight. She wasn't fond of the heights. The movie didn't help either."

I followed Yolanda to the door, feeling grateful that I had no need to take my jacket with me.

"What movie was it?" She asked as we walked into the hall.

"2012." I scoffed out.

She threw her head back and cackled. It lasted until we were nearly in the lobby again. She pulled herself together enough to explain how that was our common area. I paid better attention to the room this time. There were couches, chairs, dining tables, pool tables, foosball tables, and vending machines sporadically laid around the room. The coloring was red and white, the school colors. The mascot even had a place on one of the walls, some type of hawk I believed.

"So where are we going? Where is it safest to do this?"

"There is a park not too far from here. It has some forestry and hiking trails. I prefer to Uber there, that way it won't look as weird. Plus, it takes 20 minutes just by car. Once classes get started, I schedule to come down on the weekends. You can join me if you want. Then we can run together."

Once a week, that was going to be rough. Pat and I used to run together almost every night.

Sorry. I told my wolf.

She had been fairly silent all day. While she didn't disagree that leaving home would be a nice change, she didn't want to leave our pack either. This was not going to help matters.

It is what it is. Once a week is better than nothing.

True. I'll see what I can do about coming more often.

"So, do you know of any other… members at the school?"

We were starting to load into the mini-suv, this driver was a human guy that smelled like stale cigarettes. I had to watch what I said just in case he was listening.

"There's usually a few around campus. The local congregation is always welcoming. I've hung out at a few of their get-togethers. You may see a few from other states and areas around campus. As you would expect, they are always happy to see another member."

I nodded my understanding but kept my lips sealed. It was a good thing too. It was becoming obvious that our driver was the kind who paid close attention to his passengers' conversations. Yolanda seemed to have picked up on it as well, hence the religious turn our own conversation took.

We spent the rest of the ride in silence, rather than trying to speak in code. We barely met two hours ago; we didn't know each other well enough yet to be able to carry on a conversation in a roundabout kind of way.

The park wasn't much, at least not compared to the mountain range I was raised in. It was enough to serve our needs though.

I followed Yolanda to a small area filled with trees. She showed me the best spot to hide our backpacks, which we brought to keep our clothes clean. Neither of us were interested in getting arrested for streaking before the new semester even started.

We spent the next half hour letting our wolves run free, adjusting to the new place. Well, mine had to adjust. The smells were more than a little different. The air wasn't quite as fresh as the mountains back home, as Seattle had more pollution than we did.

Yolanda was a tawny wolf, slightly smaller than mine. Seeing as her human side was two inches shorter, that was no surprise. I did half expect her to have a small patch of purple mixed in with her tawny fur. Sadly, she didn't. I wished it had. It would have looked pretty cool.

I was stumped on what happened to all of her piercings. I wanted to ask if I could search the fur around her ears, but I figured her wolf didn't know me well enough to be comfortable with that.

I'd seen a few female shifters who pierced their ears but had never seen them in wolf form. My mom never had hers pierced and neither had I. It just seemed a little weird. Wouldn't the hole get bigger, while in wolf form, and the earring fall out?

The trip to Target took longer than the run had. I picked out a light blue bed set, and some red throw pillows. Yolanda suggested I get just the one bed set as doing laundry in the dorm laundry room was a nightmare as it was. Besides, I had no space to keep any extra bedding in my closet.

As she was more experienced at dorm life than I was, I followed her lead.

We also picked up a few essentials for the small fridge. Bread, Milk, bagels, sandwich meats, cheese, and a handful each of the small bowls of cereal. Neither of us wanted to have to worry about dishes. We even picked up paper cups and silverware. She did love my idea of the toaster oven, so we grabbed one of those as well.

We had fun laughing and talking about random things, sharing stories from home and previous years in school. We even stopped in the hair supply section. Yolanda debated whether she should change her color again. Most wolves were the same color as the hair they had as a human, so I at least had a pretty good idea of what her natural color was.

"What color was yours called? That's a pretty color." She asked as she looked through various boxes of blonde.

"Huh? What color of my what?" I may have zoned out for a second, trying to imagine her with her natural brown.

"'Your hair, silly. I love it. Is it a basic platinum? Or did you mix a black and blonde?"

"Oh!" I felt stupid. It wasn't like it was the first time I was asked this question. I grinned at her triumphantly. "Sweetheart," I picked up a lock of my loose hair with two fingers. "This here is aaall natural. Didn't you notice my fur?"

Yolanda tilted her head, her eyes showing she was thinking about it. "Huh. No, I didn't think much about it. I just assumed you were a light blonde. So, your hair really is platinum?"

She stepped over to me and started looking through my hair, probably searching for different color roots.

I giggled. "Ya huh. It's kind of cool, right? My mom is like blonde-blonde, practically white. My dad is a deep black. My brother and sister came out with a light black, almost a dark brown, but I came out with this. Since I'm the baby, I've always been the treasure." I gave her a proud grin.

"I am so jealous. Never, I repeat, never, color your hair. I will kill you in your sleep if you mess this up."

I shook my head as she went back to the shelves. "Don't worry, I don't plan on it. My whole pack would kill me."

Yolanda eventually gave up and decided to stick with purple for now. Personally, I liked it. Her hair was a dark purple, almost looking blue in some lighting. From what I had learned of her so far, I thought it fit her personality perfectly.

Using my fourth Uber for the day, we returned to our dorm. Our home for the next year. Yolanda put the few cold items we had in the minifridge, while I made my bed. We ordered a pizza for dinner, neither of us up for another trip out.

After dinner, we both crashed.

Tomorrow was Sunday, and she promised to show me around campus. Classes would start early Monday morning. Thankfully, my schedule had been emailed to me after I finished registering for classes. She also promised to take me by the book store so I could buy my books.

I told my parents that I could get a job to help pay for everything, just as I did every year back home, but they insisted that I should focus on my studies instead. I was tempted to get a job anyway, just for the experience. That, and out of state schools were more expensive. I felt a little guilty about that, seeing as it was my idea and all.

CHAPTER 3

Eric

After a quick goodbye to my parents and brother, and all the pack members who showed up to slow down my hasty exit, I left for my last year of college. The day before classes started.

I was cutting it close, but I really didn't care. The week of classes was all syllabi and expectations. That was easy, the syllabus for each class would tell me everything I missed. As for expectations, do your work and don't miss class. Duh. Any moron knew that.

Prior to last year, I only took online courses. It had worked out well, allowing me to spend time traveling to some of our neighboring packs at the same time. The typical thing for a future Alpha. It was one of the ways we maintained our relationships with them. It was tradition.

There were too many packs in the world though, so we only focused on the ones in our region. The ones who we would call for aid if something went wrong. Or who would be calling us. The ones we needed the stronger ties with.

Last thing we wanted was to return to the time of pack wars.

Besides trying to avoid the violence, it was harder to keep our existence from the humans if there were a bunch of large wolves fighting all the time.

Another tradition, at least in our pack, was for the Alpha to also be the mayor of our little "town." We held our own version of elections every few years, just to keep the humans in the nearby town happy.

For the last two generations, it's been my family holding the mayoral title. It used to be easier. Unfortunately, some of the humans have been trying for the office lately. They claimed we'd been in power too long. They had no idea just how long though.

They weren't thrilled with the idea of me taking over soon.

That was my fault really. I may have messed around with some of their daughters as a young pup. I didn't regret it, and neither did their daughters. It was just their daddies that were complaining.

In an effort to help clean up my image and prepare for the continual growth in our human population, I decided to study Political Science in school. My father and grandfather never went to college, but things were different when they took over. The town was larger now for one - well the human side was larger. The pack had grown too, obviously, but pack wolves rarely argued over who was going to be Alpha. It was the humans that needed convincing.

I completed my undergraduate degree two years ago. I started my Master's online, but eventually decided I needed to be on campus. I needed to see new faces while I still could.

I needed to find a mate. I was running out of time.

Shifter tradition stated that when the future Alpha was 25, he took over as Alpha. Every other leadership position changed as well. One big overhaul. I picked out my Beta and Gamma years ago. Giving them time to do what they needed to in order to prepare.

In our pack, the Beta was the Deputy Mayor, and the Gamma was the Sheriff. It really wasn't hard to choose. Typically, we picked the sons of the current ones. Unless there was an important, and big enough, reason not to.

Which was the case for us last year, when my chosen Gamma, Allen Jr, found his fated mate in another pack.

Normally, the females joined their mate's pack. So that shouldn't have been a problem for Allen or me. There were, however, a few rare incidents when this changed. Like this one.

Allen's mate was the only pup of their pack Alpha. Her mate, whether chosen or fated, would take over as Alpha when he turned 25. Which meant that instead of becoming my Gamma as we had planned since we were litter mates, Allen was now set to become a pack Alpha.

I hated to see him leave, but I was happy for him and the pack. Allen was a good wolf, a strong fighter, and an even stronger leader.

There would always be a low level of stress among pack members when they got closer to the time for a new leadership to take over. See, we couldn't take on our new positions if we were not mated by the time the switch came. There was a lot of pressure on us to find our mates.

Allen's new pack had more pressure than normal. Seeing as their Alpha had only the one pup, a female. Alpha's were male. They always have been. Females could have dominant wolves, but they were never dominant enough to be an Alpha. To control, lead, and protect an entire pack. Even dominant females were often softer and nicer than the males.

That meant the pressure was on for the Alpha's daughter to either find a fated mate or choose a male worthy enough. Which was a risky move for someone in her position. A fated mate was always preferable because fate would have matched her with someone who was fit for the position. But what if she didn't find her fated mate and had to pick a chosen one? What if her chosen one was not fit after all? The whole pack would all be stuck with him.

Allen's wolf had always been more dominant than most Gamma's usually were. His wolf had always struggled with lowering himself to me. He was a good fit for Alpha. I was happy for him, even though I was sad to see him leave. His new pack was in Central Oregon. A good few hours away.

In his place as Gamma, I chose my younger brother Ricky. We picked on each other a lot as pups, we even fought a good deal of the time. But nothing would change the fact that we were brothers.

As we got older, our brotherly bond strengthened. Now, he was one of my best friends.

Ricky was my complete opposite in so many ways. Where I was loud, proud, and energetic, he was quiet, calm, and self-less. The joke used to be that we were switched at birth. He was more fitting to be the politician. Ricky even joined the police force as soon as he graduated from high school.

By choice!

He also completed his degree in Criminal Justice last year - also online. He never had a desire to be on campus in large classrooms, full of people. He thrived in low key settings. He preferred them. He always said people made too much noise when they didn't need to.

With Ricky already there, in the police station, it made sense to pick him as the future Gamma. Unfortunately, that also meant he needed to find his mate before then as well. *All* leaders, whether chosen on time or not, were supposed to already be mated by the time the new Alpha took over.

I think it had something to do with our mates calming us, leveling us out. It may also have to do with us being settled and providing a foundation of stability for the pack.

I felt bad for Ricky at times like this. He was two years younger than me. I was, in essence, giving him less time to find his mate.

I had no problems with finding a chosen mate, in fact, I almost preferred it. I wanted to have a say in who I spent my life with. I mean, I wouldn't necessarily reject a fated mate. But I was also not actively looking for her. I was looking for a female that I could care about and be happy with for the rest of my life. One who would make a good Luna for my pack.

Ricky, on the other hand, had always been of the belief that fate would provide the right one for him. He would wait for her and only her. Anytime I even tried suggesting that he find a backup plan, he scoffed at me in disgust. We used to argue over it all the time, but my younger brother had become the bigger male, both physically and emotionally, and refused to rise to my bait anymore.

I made the four-hour drive back to campus on my own, reveling in the quiet. It was my time to think things over.

My Beta, Travis, found his fated mate in high school. He was a few years older than her. Travis had his first shift at twelve, like most of us. It wasn't long after that he started hanging around a female who was three years younger, Mary. The adults had their suspicions, but they kept it from the rest of us. By the time she shifted at thirteen, we had figured out why.

I knew, for a human, the idea of a thirteen-year-old and sixteen-year-old was a bit creepy, but for wolves, it wasn't. Besides, their wolves were still maturing as well. Finding your mate when you were young was not the same as finding your mate when you were older. It was more like finding your best friend.

As soon as she turned 18, they finished the mating process. By then, Travis was 21 and working out way more than everyone else. Nobody in the pack would have blinked an eye if they had been a more *active* mating pair, it was natural in our eyes. The humans in the area though would not have been as understanding. Travis worried it would damage his political reputation with them, so he waited.

Now it was just down to Ricky and I. Travis didn't want to be Alpha, so he was also starting to be a bit annoying about it all. If neither my brother nor I found a mate, the job would fall to him to run the pack. Which he was very adamant he did not want to do.

We had less than a year left before I turned 25. We had plenty of females from our own pack to choose from, but neither of us wanted one of them. At least, I didn't any more. I already tasted the buffet from the Glacier Pack. They were fun for the moment, just not anyone I would want around long term.

Ricky… well… Ricky never even entered the buffet line. He was all about his fated mate. I truly hoped that he would find her somehow. He was a good male, a good man. He deserved the best, and I had no doubt that fate picked out the best mate for him. A female who would liven up his life in a way that would help him be comfortable in the outside world. And, at the same time, be someone who would sit back and chill with him.

I grinned as I pulled up to the small house the local pack kept for any future Alphas attending Seattle U.

While it wasn't required, typically the packs near colleges kept a place for future Alphas to stay while they attended the college. Keeping a healthy relationship with those you would be working with in the future was always a good idea.

Jordan walked out the front door as I pulled in.

It was also normal for them to go a step further and provide a pack warrior to help protect that Alpha. Nobody wanted a war, or to be held responsible if something happened to a future Alpha of another pack in their territory. The retribution would not be pretty.

Jordan was assigned to me last year when I first started on campus. I was glad to see that they kept it the same. We got along well, as did our wolves. Jordan was a year younger than me. He was studying Physical Education. The male lived for sports and being on the move. Which was one of the reasons we got along so well.

I stepped out of the car and spread my arms wide. "Jordan!"

Jordan laughed and walked toward me, with his hand stretched out to grasp mine. I pulled him into a hug, patting his back roughly with my free hand.

"About time you got here. What took so long?" He laughed some more as he walked to the trunk and pulled out my bags.

I tried to give an embarrassed smile, but he saw through it. "Well, when you're popular, everyone has to say goodbye."

Jordan shook his head. My popularity wasn't news to him. I was always the center of any crowd. It was just who I was. I loved it too.

"Well, you have just enough time to unpack and clean up. Alpha Turner and Luna Teri are expecting us for dinner tonight."

I froze in the doorway, carrying one of my bags, to our humble home for the next year. I turned and raised an eyebrow at him.

"That's new."

Jordan looked uncomfortable as he looked down at the other bag he was carrying, his freehand rubbing the back of his neck.

"Yeah, uh. They invited a few members of the pack to join us for a welcoming party."

I groaned and continued our walk inside and down the hall to my room. "Let me guess, the party list includes a variety of unmated females?"

It wasn't entirely uncommon for packs to gather them together when unmated males were visiting. Not everyone had the opportunity to search for a mate outside of their own pack. I sighed as I plopped my bag on top of the king-size bed inside the master bedroom that was mine. Jordan's room was further down the hall, closer to the guest bathroom that he used.

"I guess I should be grateful. I do need to find a mate this year. Did you hear if we got any new wolf blood on campus for this year?"

Jordan grinned. "A few more have joined us, not many but some. I don't know anything about them, only that they are here. You already know Alpha Turner will not release that information to anyone, not even you."

I gave a mock pout, then kicked his laughing rear end out of my room.

An hour later, we were back on the road, headed for my sponsoring pack. I spent time with them before, during one of my many visits in my travels. They did have many beautiful females. I made sure to spend time speaking to each of them, as was expected of me. Not that anyone would outright say that it was. It was one of those unspoken expectations in polite society. Each of them offered me their numbers, I stacked them in order of preference. Not when they were looking of course. I refused to be that much of a cad.

On the way home, Jordan gave me the third degree while he drove. "Anyone peak your interests?"

"Yes and no. I might call a few of them down the road. My wolf wasn't really interested in any of them though. If we're going to choose a mate, we have to be on the same side. And not just for harmony in the mating."

Physically mating would literally be impossible if your wolf wasn't in agreement. Both wolves were involved in the process, not completely, but enough to mark that wolf as belonging to them.

My wolf was more impatient than I was about this. Which was the only reason he was willing to go along with choosing a mate. He was an Alpha who needed a mate in order to best protect his pack.

He was a picky sucker though.

Classes started early the next morning. Jordan was kind enough to have picked up all my books for me over the weekend. I previously sent him the list of what I would need the week before. Since there wasn't any real danger around here, he sometimes acted more like an assistant than a bodyguard.

We lived close enough to campus that we were able to walk to our classes. Well, close enough for a wolf shifter. For a human it might have been too far. With so few areas to set our wolves loose, we needed the extra exercise to keep them sated. And as long as there weren't too many humans around, we could put on a little more speed into our morning jaunt to class.

Jordan arranged his schedule to walk with me to my first and last classes, and for us to have lunch together. It was a good thing I liked him, otherwise his hovering all the time would get annoying. I complained a little at the beginning of last year. I didn't want, or need, a bodyguard.

I even vented about it to my parents over Thanksgiving break. My mom, always the wise one in the home, set me straight.

"That is the life of an Alpha. It is an honor for the warrior chosen to protect the Alpha. And an even bigger honor to protect the future Alpha. Do not deny Jordan this privilege. It will give him a higher position within his own pack. Plus, it is good practice for both of you. For you, it's practice having a guard around all the time. For him, he gets to practice the skills he was taught. Help him become a better warrior by allowing him to protect you."

I wasn't happy about it, but she made a good point. I liked Jordan enough by then that I was willing to help him out and play nice. Once I let the babysitter feeling go, we got along loads better. We were able to start having more fun together too.

When we got to the Poly Sci building, Jordan patted my shoulder and laughed. "Happy hunting, my friend."

I laughed with him. Yeah, we both knew I was going to be on the hunt all day for any new female blood on campus. I had tried to nonchalantly ask Luna Teri about the new wolves on campus this year. She smiled knowingly and shook her head, refusing to answer.

You couldn't blame an unmated male for trying.

By the end of the first day, I knew that none of the new wolves were in my department. I was the only wolf there.

I did catch a few scents around campus that week, some I recognized from the year previously, and some I didn't recognize at all. I was crossing my fingers that they weren't all male.

By Friday, I was exhausted. The studying time for each class was already killing me. My focus was on Comparative Political Economy. Which meant my classes tended to focus on the economy. Out of all my choices, I figured that would benefit my pack and town the most.

I was beginning to miss the classes that took longer to get to the dirty stuff.

I did end up adding an English class this year, figuring that one had to be common enough that another wolf would be in there. Which there were. Three of them as a matter of fact.

Unfortunately, there were also 50 humans in there with us. The class had already been full when I got there, so the scents were all mixed together. It was even worse when everyone walked out together. I was mostly certain who two of the wolves were, both males. The third one, not so much. Not one stinking clue.

Jordan was still working on his generals, as well as his major classes, so he was as tired as me. We both collapsed on the couch that afternoon, our feet spread out in front of us, our heads hanging off the back. Neither of us were exactly tiny.

Jordan was an inch shorter than me, coming in around 6'2. He was wider though, which was common amongst warrior wolves. I trained along with ours, just not as often in recent years. Jordan actually reminded me of that werewolf kid from the *Twilight* movies.

I only knew what he looked like because the females I dated in high school insisted I take them to see the movies when they came out. And every time I swore the next female would not convince me to sit through that again. I was wrong every time. The rewards always outweighed the consequences though. So, it was worth it in the end.

Between the two of us, Jordan and I enveloped nearly the entire six-foot couch. We laid like that for a good ten minutes before either of us spoke.

"You up for a party? The football players are having their season kickoff party tonight."

I huffed. Those buffoons always had a reason to party. For a species that couldn't hold their liquor very well, they sure drank every chance they got. I shouldn't talk though. I went to nearly every party last year. And won every drinking game I entered.

I sighed and leaned forward, placing my elbows on my knees, clasping my hands together.

"Not tonight. I'm too tired."

Jordan gave a deeply relieved sigh, making me chuckle. "Yes! Finally! I am so glad you don't want to go."

Poor pup. I wondered how many parties he went to last year out of duty. I needed to keep that in mind. I already knew he would never refuse to go or talk me out of going, unless there was danger involved.

As much as I hated to admit it, we probably needed to do fewer parties this year. Any female who would make a decent Luna was not going to be hitting up frat parties and getting drunk with friends.

I pushed myself up to a standing position. "I'm ordering pizza. Maybe after dinner we can start coming up with ways to find the new females, without hitting up every party on campus this year."

Jordan lifted a weak arm in a cheer, then dropped it on his chest. "I like that plan. Wake me when the pizza gets here."

I laughed as his eyes closed and the snoring started a minute later. Poor pup. At least my classes were more mentally exhausting than physically exhausting.

CHAPTER 4

Cassie

My first week of school was a success. I absolutely loved being there. The classes were similar to the ones I took in Anchorage. I lived for the deep discussions we had with the professors. The other students were a mix of snobs, nerds, and wallflowers. I was a mix of the last two.

At least I thought I was. No one had ever called me a snob before, so I was sure I was safe. I hoped so anyway.

I enjoyed getting involved with the class discussions, but I also liked to sit back and listen to what everyone else had to say. Along with my psychology classes, I had a few pre-med classes I still needed to take.

I took my Physics Lab last year, the one I had dreaded the most. Pat and I took it together. He had put it off as long as he could. I would have as well, but he talked me into taking it with him. All I had left of my pre-med courses was Organic Chemistry and English.

On Wednesday, Yolanda took me to this little mom and pop Cafe a block away from campus. It was adorable. The food was really good too. We did notice that the lady who owned the place was looking a bit haggard when she came to refill our waters.

"Everything alright, Marybelle? You look a little tired." I asked softly.

Marybelle was a sweet older lady, one that looked like she had lived a happy life and was nearly ready to retire.

She gave me a soft smile, the kind that said it was sweet of me to ask. "I'll be alright, darling. Usually, we have our staff for the new year hired before school starts. Unfortunately, one of our waitresses had a family emergency and couldn't return this year. Now I have to search for a new waitress all over again. Until then, I will be doing double duty."

Yolanda and I looked at each other. She lifted her eyes and moved her lips in a "it's worth a shot" look. We had brainstormed ideas for a job a few times since Saturday.

I cleared my throat nervously, looking at the table. I'd never looked for a job before. I wasn't sure how to do this. The jobs I worked back home had all been through the pack. No real applying needed.

"I was hoping to find a job for the year. I don't exactly have any experience waiting tables, but I am a fast learner, and I am really good with people. I grew up helping my parents in their clinic."

Marybelle tilted her head and studied me for a minute. Just long enough for me to think she was going to say no.

"Can you work evenings? What's your class schedule like?"

My eyes widened. "Uh, yeah. My classes are out by three, most days. Earlier on Fridays."

"Perfect. As long as you can keep up with the work, and don't break all my dishes, or spill things on the customers, we should be fine. I'll be back with the paperwork. You can start your training tomorrow."

I squealed with glee as soon as she disappeared into the kitchen. Yolanda high fived me across the table. And just like that, I had a job. I thought for sure it was going to take me longer to find something.

Like she said, they usually had their staffing done before classes started. I figured that would be the story everywhere.

I worked every day the rest of the week, and all weekend. Marybelle scheduled me to work evenings on Saturdays and Sundays, giving me most of the day to catch up on studying. I caught on quickly to how things worked at the Cafe, and I absolutely loved it.

I loved interacting with all the different customers. I liked being on my feet and on the move. My wolf especially liked the on the move part. She never cared much for sitting in classes all day long.

She knew *why* we did it, she just didn't *like* to do it.

Marybelle was also helping me feel a little less homesick. Her no nonsense attitude, mixed with her compassion, reminded me of my mom. The cafe was quickly beginning to feel like family. My human family.

The human males were always flirty. I met a few of the other wolves on campus as well. It seemed working allowed me to meet more people, go figure. The males were kind of cute, and a little protective when the human ones started getting flirty. It was kind of sweet and always made me laugh. It wasn't like they hadn't been acting much better.

No matter the pack or level of dominance, male wolves were always territorial of female wolves. Their wolf counterpart insisted on it.

I hadn't given much thought to finding a mate while I was gone. With Pat always being the overprotective brother hanging around me, dating really wasn't much of an option. Maybe I could this year. It would be kind of fun. Especially without him hanging over my shoulder every minute.

I had a few classes with other wolves. Mainly my English and Chemistry classes. I wasn't surprised. There was one male that I had in both, we became friends and sat together each time. It helped soothe our wolves with all the humans around.

Tristan was in his first year, still barely a pup. I felt like I needed to watch out for him. He was more submissive than me, and his wolf was a little scared of the large crowd in the classrooms. I always wondered what it would be like to have a little brother. Now I knew.

Hopefully he didn't prove to be as much of a deterrent as Pat always was.

On my second Friday night working, two wolves I hadn't met yet walked through the door. One of them smelled familiar. I thought he might be in my English class as well, so I took a second to take him in.

He was taller than me, maybe even taller than Pat. He was about average build for a wolf, which was above average for a human. His friend was close in height but bigger in width. One had blondish hair, the other had black hair. The blonde was paler than the other. My wolf took interest in him as well. He would make for a fine mate one day. He would take good care of his mate. A strong protector.

While she would prefer a fated mate, we both knew and accepted the odds a long time ago. Her main concern was finding a wolf that would be someone we could depend on. A provider. A protector. This one carried that trait in his body language.

I approached the table, both of their eyes shooting to me as soon as they caught my scent. Their lips spread into large grins, while their eyes raked over my body. I rolled my eyes.

We would also prefer someone who wasn't a douche.

"Good evening, gentlemen. Can I get you started off with something to drink?" I smiled kindly, like any good waitress.

The blonde one couldn't take his eyes off me. The dark-haired one kicked him under the table. I was assuming that was what happened at least. As the blonde jerked and shook his head.

"Water for now, thank you." He said, before clearing his throat awkwardly.

His friend laughed and asked for water as well.

"Alright. I'll be right back. Menus are right there," I pointed at the laminated menus that were kept in a medal holder on one end of the table, "take a look and tell me when you're ready to order."

CHAPTER 5

Eric

I groaned pitifully and dropped my head to the table, feeling completely embarrassed. Never in my life had I ever frozen when confronted by a female. Ever!

Jordan was laughing like it was the best show on earth. I lifted one hand and flipped him off. Which made him laugh harder.

"I take it we like this one?"

I lifted my head back up and watched the waitress filling two glasses with water. I cleared my throat as she bent over to pick up something from the lower shelf. Those jeans she was wearing shaped her butt perfectly.

Even my wolf had paid attention when her scent first hit us.

I like this one. She smells strong. He told me.

That she does, my friend. She smells familiar. Do you recognize it?

Yes. She is in that class with us. The one we don't need. The one you'd fail if I wasn't paying attention while you slept.

I huffed at him. I wanted to argue, but I couldn't. I found the class boring. I studied her hair, placing her. Then it hit me. I'd seen her sitting with one of the male pups in class.

Do you think the pup is her mate?

No, I can't smell any other wolf on her. She is unmated.

Perfect.

"How does your wolf feel about this one?" Jordan was still smiling, pushing for an answer, and probably knowing that we had just been discussing her.

I looked back at him, hopefully *before* she had turned around and caught me staring.

"He agrees."

That was all I had time for before she was back with our drinks.

"Did you gentlemen decide what you would like yet? Or do you need more time?"

I know what I want.

My wolf was not helping me here. Normally he didn't get involved much when it came to the females. Just enough to say yay or nay. As long as I didn't try to mark any of them, he didn't care what I did.

Me too, but we have to play this cool. We don't want to scare her off.

He gave me a small growl and I chuckled. Which did not go unnoticed by the pretty waitress. She raised an eyebrow at me. I held my breath, not sure how she would respond.

"I take it you are having an internal debate. Maybe we should start you off with a nice big *salad*. I'm sure that would hit the spot." Her eyes twinkled with amusement.

Don't you dare. My wolf argued. I could feel his amusement at her teasing. He was enjoying this as much as I was.

I smiled at her. "I think we better stick with the meat for now. I'll keep that in mind though just in case I need to prove a point."

Jordan and I ordered double bacon cheeseburgers, fully loaded, with large plates of cheese fries for each. Jordan waited until she was in the kitchen before speaking softly. Who knew how good her hearing was?

"Guess we need a different set of plans. That didn't take long. She's not going to make it easy for you though."

I smiled and shook my head. "That's what makes her perfect. If I wanted something easy, I would have chosen someone from home."

I rotated my position in our booth, allowing myself to watch her through most of the restaurant, and studied her unabashedly as she walked around to all her tables, talking to customers and cleaning up after them.

The female had long beautiful legs. Her body was toned. Her skin looked like melted caramel. Her hair was blonde, yet it was so light, it almost looked like she had platinum colored hair. Her eyes were a light blue, and they shimmered with silver when she smiled. She had an exotic beauty to her. Something I had never seen before.

I didn't even bother trying to hide my desire this time when she returned with our food. How could anyone not watch a masterpiece when they were in its presence?

When her eyes met mine, a small blush crept up her cheeks. I didn't think anything could enhance her beauty. I was happy to be wrong.

She set the plates down in front of us. "Can I get you males anything else?"

I chuckled. "Yeah, your name would be great."

She smiled at me and lowered her head for a split second. "Cassie. And you two are?"

"I'm Eric, this is my roommate Jordan."

There was no way I was about to call him my bodyguard. I rarely ever did. I wanted her to like me for me, not because of who I was. One of the many reasons I didn't choose one of the females from my own pack. They were after the position more than they were after me.

"Nice to meet you both. Enjoy your meals."

She turned on her heels and left so fast I couldn't even think of what else to say to keep her there. I looked up when I heard Jordan trying not to laugh again. I raised a questioning eyebrow, and he lost control.

"It's nice to see even the smooth-talking Alpha can get tongue tied around a pretty female."

I flipped him off again. "Shut up." I grumbled. Which just made him laugh harder. Along with my wolf.

Maybe you should let me do all the talking. We are never going to catch this female at this rate.

You can shut up too.

When she came back, Jordan decided to help me out.

"So, Cassie. Where are you from?"

"Alaska."

"Really?" I asked. I hadn't met anyone from Alaska before. Their packs were closed off from most of the world. "Are you an eskimo then?"

Her eyes narrowed at me. Why did I feel like I said something wrong?

Jordan jumped in, right as her foot was turning to leave.

"I apologize for my friend. He didn't mean any offense. He's not from around these parts either." Jordan's intense stare met my confused one. "He didn't know that was a derogatory comment." His last bit came out slow, emphasizing each syllable, with his eyes getting wider, making sure I understood what he was saying.

I did. I just insulted the first female my wolf and I both agreed on. The most beautiful creature to have ever walked this earth. My wolf cursed at me, and I covered my face with my hand.

"I am so sorry, Cassie. I truly had no idea." I looked up into her eyes. They were still slightly narrowed at me but softening. "Let me make it up to you?"

Now they were narrowing in a "you gotta be kidding me" kind of way. "And exactly how are you going to do that?"

I thought carefully, I knew absolutely nothing about this woman. Except where she worked, where she was from, and that I deeply offended her.

I had a light bulb moment and turned to her with a smile. "I could take all your notes in English for the next week."

I should be offended by how hard her, Jordan, and my wolf were laughing at that offer. I couldn't be though. My wolf was practically humming with the beautiful sound coming from her. The tension in her eyes was gone, and her eyes were shining. I tried to scowl, even though I wasn't feeling it.

"No offense, Eric. But you'd have to stay awake in order to take those notes."

I winked at her. "So, you've noticed me then."

She guffawed while holding her lips closed tightly. "Honey, everyone noticed. Did you know you snore?"

Jordan fell onto the bench laughing.

"I do not!" I argued back, fighting the smile.

"Yes, you do." They both said in unison.

I grumbled, playing along. She could make fun of me every day and I would be happy.

Yes, she will make a good Luna and keep us in line. Keep us humble.

I couldn't agree more.

"Fine, how about this. Jordan is from the local pack. He knows of a great place to go for a run. Are you free tomorrow? You can come with us. I bet your wolf is dying to get free."

Cassie rubbed her lips together and eyed me carefully. She let her eyes roam freely up and down my body. She knew as well as I did, this wasn't just a run with a new friend. My wolf preened under her scrutiny, dying to get out and show her our real strength.

"Fine, but only because my roommate and I were planning on running anyway. We go every Saturday."

I couldn't help the grin spreading on my face. "It's a date then." I stood up and winked at her, throwing all the cash I had in my pocket on the table. I didn't even bother counting it first.

"No, it's a run. That's it." She tried to be firm, pointing at me with her adorable little finger, but her eyes were deceiving her. They were sparkling with excitement.

"Whatever you say, sweetheart." I may have gotten a little too bold. I put my hand on her waist and leaned down to kiss her cheek softly. "Meet us in the quad at eight."

Cassie's breath caught as soon as my fingers touched her. Her eyes closed when my lips brushed her skin. Oh yeah, she was definitely mine.

Jordan and I left the cafe we had randomly stopped in for dinner, both of us had wanted something different tonight, neither of said anything until after the drive home. As soon as the front door closed behind us, I lifted my arms in the air and shouted. Jordan laughed then patted me on the back.

"Don't start planning the mating yet my friend. Now the real work begins."

I scoffed. "Work. This isn't going to be work. That female is as good as mine."

"Maybe for now. But what if she is waiting for her fated mate? Many females leave home for school, hoping to find them."

I swatted the air as though I could push his concerns away. I certainly didn't have any. "Nah. Cassie is as good as mine. She was as affected by me as I was by her."

Jordan snorted as he headed for his room. "Nope, her brain never malfunctioned. Yours did. I got homework. I'll see you in the morning."

I let him close his door and get to studying. That had been our plan for tonight after all. I had been contemplating ordering pizza again, but Jordan reminded me that I needed to leave the house to find my mate. And he was sick of pizza.

I was so glad that I listened to him. I mostly did because last year he wouldn't have had the guts to speak up, I was proud of him.

I closed my own door and sat down at my desk. I tried to force my brain to focus, but it wasn't working. My wolf wasn't helping much either. He kept bringing up images of Cassie and how good she smelled.

I closed my book, giving up after only ten minutes, and picked up my phone. I was too happy to study.

"I'm surprised you're not out at a party somewhere tonight." The gruff voice answered on the other end.

"Wow, is that how you greet your big brother? I'm not sure I want to talk to you anymore."

Ricky laughed from the other end. "Seriously, man. What's up? Last year you never missed a party on a Friday night. Bored already?"

"With the parties? Yeah, a bit."

"Woah. That was a big jump. Did the growth spurt into manhood hurt? Did you pull a muscle?"

"Shut up or I'm hanging up." Ricky continued to laugh until he could take a steading breath.

"Are you good now?" I was already getting irritated with his harassment. I knew that I liked to party last year, and every year really, but still.

"Yeah, yeah. So, what's going on? I don't usually hear from you so soon into the year. Everything alright over there?"

I smiled. This was why I called. "Everything's perfect, Ric."

The line was quiet for just a moment while he processed this. "You found a mate."

My brother knew me well.

"Yes, sir. I did. She's perfect too. I can't wait to bring her home. You're going to love her. She was razing me right from the start."

Ricky chuckled lightly. "I hate to ask, but you know I have to."

"She's chosen. I just met Cassie tonight. The connection was strong. I'm a little surprised she's not my fated, actually."

I really was too. With such a strong immediate attraction, it would have made sense for her to be. If I wasn't so well versed in the signs, I would have assumed she was. I had no doubts that had Cassie been my fated mate, I would have practically mounted her right there in the restaurant.

"If you just met her, how can you be sure? You don't know what she wants yet."

I rolled my eyes, and my head. He really should have been the older brother. He was so bossy and mature all the time.

"You sound like Jordan. Trust me, Ricky. She's it. She's the one I've been looking for."

He gave a sad sigh and let the subject drop. We were never going to see eye to eye on this one. He would understand when he met her. Cassie was everything. Cassie was it.

"Well, tell me about my future sister-in-law. What you know anyway."

I ignored his attitude, too happy to care, and told him everything that happened. I told him about her platinum hair and her shapely…legs. I could hear him smack his head when I mentioned my faux pax and heard him laugh about the salad thing.

"I'm glad you found someone that makes you this happy, Eric. Let me know how things go tomorrow?"

"I will. Hey, let mom and dad know, will ya? I really should try to get some studying done tonight."

We said goodnight and got off the phone. Talking to my brother about things always helped me to settle my mind. He was a good brother, a good friend. I didn't know what I would do without him. I even managed to get a paper written for my political theory class done, after talking to him.

CHAPTER 6

Cassie

I walked on air for the rest of my shift. Eric was fun, he was handsome, and he was kind. A bit full of himself, but what male wasn't? No matter the species.

He was lucky it was me he made that comment too. If he had said it to one of the males in my pack, there would have been a fight right then.

What was your take on him? I asked my wolf. She'd been oddly quiet the whole night. She usually liked to put her two cents into things.

He's strong, and an Alpha. I will withhold further judgment until I meet his wolf.

Well, I guess it's a good thing we are going for a run tomorrow.

Yes, I hope this place they are taking us is better than where we've been. That park is too cramped.

It's the best I can do for now.

I know.

I rolled my eyes. Guess she was still holding a bit of a grudge about us leaving. She would forgive me, especially if we got a mate out of it.

We'll see.

I finished my shift and headed back to the dorms. It was late, so the place was quiet. Unlike human females, I didn't have a problem walking alone in the dark. I was stronger than your average human male. Faster than the above average ones too. My eyesight worked a bit better than theirs as well.

Yolanda was laying on her bed, reading a textbook, when I walked in.

"Hey. How was work?" She asked without even lifting her head up.

I bit my lip, realizing I probably should have asked her about tomorrow, before roping her into it without her permission. My pause was long enough that she set down her highlighter and looked up.

"Cas? What happened?"

"I...uh. I met someone tonight."

Yolanda sat up, folding her legs under her. "This is shaping up to be a good story. Spill it, sister."

I set my backpack on top of my desk and sat down in the hard back chair that came with it. I told her the story of my night, leaving off the plans for the morning.

"Oh, Cas, that's great. I'm so happy for you. I know we haven't really talked about this, but how do you feel about the whole fated versus chosen thing?"

I shrugged and started taking my shoes off. "A fated mate would be ideal, of course. In Alaska though, we are so far removed from the rest of the shifter population, that finding your fated mate is even rarer for us. The majority of wolves usually choose their mate. My parents got lucky since my mom was on vacay when she met my dad. So, while I would love to find that one wolf who was created just for me, I can't spend my whole life holding out for him to find me."

Yolanda nodded her head sadly. "I get it. I can't decide, myself. I can't help but think I would always have doubts if I chose someone. What if I cut that bond, and then the next day my fated shows up? I would never know because the bond would be gone. What if I chose poorly, and they had hidden who they really were from me until it was too late. I would have bonded myself permanently to a mate I should have never chosen."

I nodded my head. I got what she was saying. I had the same fears.

"I worry about the same things, Yo. We can't let fear of the unknown rule our lives though. Besides, just because someone is fated for you, doesn't mean that it is the right fit either. There is always a pair that never should have gotten together. Mostly because one of the mates made some very bad choices."

Yolanda sighed. "That's true enough. Anyway, enough with the depressing. When are you seeing Eric again?"

I licked my lips and looked down at my hands folded in my lap. "About that. I sort of agreed for you and me to go running with him and his roommate tomorrow. Jordan is from the Olympic pack, and he knows of a good place to go. I didn't want to go just me and them, so I kind of included you in the deal. You aren't mad are you?"

She laughed. "Do I wish you had asked me first? Obviously. Mad though? No. I would have said yes, because you shouldn't be alone with two males we don't know, in the woods. Or anywhere for that matter."

I leaned over and gave her a hug, thanking her. We talked a little more, I gave her every detail about both Jordan and Eric. According to Eric, it was a date. Which meant, it was technically a double date.

It took me a while to get to sleep, and when I did, I dreamed about a sandy colored wolf chasing me through the forests. When he caught me, we wrestled and played together in the moonlight. At one point, he had me pinned below him. I shifted back to my skin, and he followed my lead. I smiled up at the male as he lowered down to kiss me.

I woke up the next morning with a big smile on my face. It wasn't until I was putting my shoes on that I realized it hadn't been Eric in my dream. The male in my dream looked similar to him, but he had darker hair, and his facial features weren't as rough as Eric's.

Huh. Weird.

Whatever, it didn't matter. I had only met Eric the one time. It made sense that my dream version of him would not be a perfect replica. There were enough similarities in there that I could believe that.

Yolanda and I walked out of the dorm building and down to the quad in silence. I saw her hands twisting, feeling just as nervous as me. Which was odd. I'd never seen her nervous, not even on the first day of school. I thought about asking her what was up, but I soon saw two male figures standing under the trees.

The wind shifted and I caught Eric's scent.

I smiled to myself and sped up, he started walking toward me as well, a cheesy grin on his face. I was so caught up in Eric, I barely noticed that Yolanda was slowing down, almost like I was dragging her along with me, against her will.

"Good morning." Eric greeted me, kissing my cheek once again.

"Good morning." I wasn't really sure how to respond, so I settled for good manners and turned to introduce my roommate.

"This is my roommate, Yolanda." I waved to her as I glanced back at her. Then I stopped talking and looked again.

Eric noticed the way she froze as well, her eyes not leaving Jordan's. We looked over at Jordan whose jaw was on the ground. Neither of them were speaking or moving. I giggled and moved behind Yolanda. Her wolf must have felt him nearby, that was probably why she had been so jittery this morning.

I gave her a small push toward Jordan. "Yolanda, this is Jordan. Jordan, Yolanda."

Eric walked over to his roommate at the same time and used one finger under his jaw to close his mouth. Which served to help pull Jordan out of his trance. His grin was slow but very, very happy. Yolanda's answering one, was shy. I didn't even know she knew how to be shy.

"Good morning, beautiful." Jordan said softly, lifting his palm to her cheek.

She leaned into it, her wolf practically purring in her chest. "Good morning."

Jordan took one tentative step forward, bringing himself closer to her. Yolanda seemed to gain some of her normal personality back. She reached up to the back of his neck and pulled him down to her height. His grin widened even more as she met him halfway.

"Well then." Eric said, in a very uncomfortable way. He turned toward a bench nearby, pointing at it. "Shall we give them a minute?"

I giggled, glancing back at our roommates. "We probably should. Just to be nice."

We sat down on the bench, trying not to look at the way my roommate was wrapping herself around her fated mate.

"This isn't getting awkward." Eric laughed awkwardly, turning himself to face me.

"It's sweet, and probably long overdue. Yolanda has been coming here for years. It's about time they met."

Eric shrugged, raising his arm over the back of the bench, letting his fingers play with my hair.

"Timing is everything. They probably weren't ready before now."

"Maybe." I shivered as I felt his fingers begin to trail along my neck. I leaned away just enough for his fingers to fall. "You can scratch those ideas right out of your head, mister. They are fated, we are not. You have to slow down."

Eric grinned, laughing quietly at me. When he didn't argue with me, or reach for me again, I relaxed and straightened back up.

His fingers went right back to my hair.

"Are you waiting for fate, Cassie?" His voice was deep, a slight tremor telling me this was an important question he needed to ask.

I met his eyes carefully. "Not necessarily. My home is isolated. It's not often a wolf finds their fated one. Chosen mates are more common. Even our Alpha has a chosen mate."

I closed my eyes as his fingers slid behind my head, his palm covering one of my ears. I knew that I should move away again, but it felt really really nice.

Eric's voice was softer this time, and… closer. I opened my eyes and realized his face was inches from mine.

"You are open to a chosen mate then?"

"Yes, I would never rush it though." My voice was raspier than I had ever heard it.

His eyes flashed to my lips and then up to my eyes again. "I can live with that."

Before I could take another breath, his lips were on mine. I'd only kissed a few other males in my time. All back when I was in high school, where Pat was unable to cock block me, or lip block, in my case.

I groaned as I felt Eric's arm slide around my waist, pulling me closer. It was a good few minutes before we parted again, both of us with cheesy grins.

Half an hour later, the four of us finally left for our run.

Eric insisted on driving, telling Jordan to sit in the back with his mate. Neither of them argued.

The drive took about an hour, but it was a pleasant drive. The males had planned a trip to Mount Vernon for us. The drive was filled with laughter and lots of talking. We took the opportunity for all of us to get to know each other better.

Our wolves enjoyed the run through the mountains. Eric's wolf was a gorgeous dirty blonde color. Jordan's a dark gray. Not long after we got started, Yolanda's wolf took off running, testing her mate. Eric and I laughed, watching Jordan take off after her.

While Yolanda made her mate earn her affections, Eric and I ran and let our wolves play until we reached a stream. Then we let our wolves play in the water. I had no doubts that Eric would have loved for me to shift back and swim in the water. But I wasn't ready for that yet.

Thankfully, he followed my lead and stayed in his wolf form as well. Neither of our wolves complained.

As we had no familial connection, thankfully, and no pack connection, nor were we mated, Eric and I had no way to actually communicate. Our wolves seemed to do okay with body language and stuff, I wasn't thrilled with it though. Hopefully in time I would learn to be able to read his cues better.

The drive home was quieter, we were all tired. Our wolves were relaxed and content after a few hours of running free. Eric went through a drive thru on the way back, getting lunch for all of us. He drove us straight up to our dorms, then opened my door for me. Yolanda and I both got some heart melting farewell kisses.

We both grinned at each other as we walked inside and took the elevator up. It wasn't until our door was closed that the squealing began. We both jumped up and down, flapping our arms and hands in front of us like we were birds and not wolves. We ended with a big hug.

"Congratulations! I am so happy for you!"

"Thank you!" Yolanda sat on her bed, a dumbfounded look on her face. "When I woke up this morning, my wolf was pacing. I had a feeling something was going to happen. I just didn't know what it was. Then his scent hit me like a semi-truck going fifty over the speed limit." She gave a contented sigh then looked up at me. "Should I be saying congratulations to you as well. You and Eric seemed pretty content together."

I laughed and sat down next to her, taking her hand in mine. "I really like him, Yo. I'm not ready to commit to anything yet, but I could see myself choosing him. Way, way down the road."

Yolanda laid her head on my shoulder. "I half expected you and Jordan to come out of those woods fully mated." I teased.

I felt her shake her head before lifting it again. "We discussed it and decided to wait until the semester is over. One of the reasons he was picked for this assignment was because he was unmated. He needs to give his Alpha time to find a replacement for his spot."

I pulled my eyebrows together, totally confused at what she was saying. "What assignment?"

"Didn't they tell you? Jordan isn't just Eric's roommate, he's his bodyguard."

"Bodyguard? Why?"

Yolanda bit the corner of her lip, looking worried. "Maybe it's not my business to tell you."

"Yeah, you're definitely going to have to tell me now."

She sighed. "Eric is a future Alpha. Alpha Turner, the Olympic Alpha, assigned Jordan the task of being his bodyguard. They've become really good friends too. It's all just a precaution obviously. There hasn't been a pack war, or even a rogue attack in these parts in decades."

I nodded, yeah, that made sense.

I felt my heart deflate, my joy from moments before seeping out through my pores. Alphas rarely settled for a chosen mate. Eric had made it sound like he wanted one though. My wolf had even said the day before that he was an Alpha, but I guess it hadn't fully sunk in.

I didn't even realize when the tears started falling. Yolanda saw them first and pulled me into a hug. She spent the next little bit soothing me and trying to build me back up. I felt a little guilty, seeing as how we should be celebrating that she found her fated mate today.

Thankfully, before long, I had to get ready for work. I welcomed the distraction. Saturday nights were always busy, and tonight was no different.

Ten minutes before closing Eric walked in and sat on a stool at the bar.

"What are you doing here?" I mentally slapped myself for letting it sound like an accusation.

Eric didn't miss it either. His voice sounded unsure, like maybe he read me wrong. Which he didn't since he only had my behavior that morning to go off of. Which, let's be honest here, was sending all the right signals. I mean, okay, I said the whole kissing thing wasn't going to happen and yet he did it anyway. But I didn't exactly stop him either.

"I thought I would give you a lift home. Everything alright?"

I nodded and turned away. I could feel the traitorous tears fighting for a way out. I sniffed. "Yeah, I'm fine. Just give me a few minutes."

It was good he was there. I could interrogate him now instead of waiting until later, after I lost sleep going over every little thing in my head and stressing over it all.

He waited patiently, with a very worried expression. It was kind of sweet. I pushed my apron under the bar and grabbed my purse. Neither of us said anything until we were both in the car.

"What's wrong, Cassie?"

"How old are you, Eric?"

"Uh...24. Why? I really don't think I'm that much older than you."

I shook my head. That meant he had less than a year to find a mate. "Did you just pick me because I'm one of the few females around and you are getting desperate for a mate?"

He didn't even hesitate when he answered vehemently. "Hell, no! I picked you because you're the first female to challenge me, you have a sassy mouth, you care about others, and you are the most beautiful female I have ever seen."

"So, it has nothing to do with you becoming Alpha in a year?"

His head fell, ashamed. I nodded once, taking that as my answer, and started opening the door to just walk home. I was barely lifting the handle when he reached over me and pulled my hand away again.

"No, my timeline had nothing to do with it. Yes, I have been searching for a mate. I've never cared whether she was a fated mate or a chosen mate. Frankly, I can't imagine a fated one getting any better than you." Eric placed a gentle hand on my cheek and guided my face to look at his.

"Why didn't you tell me you were a future Alpha?" My voice cracked, letting the hurt I still felt show.

"Because I wanted you to like me for me, not for what I am." His voice was soft and a little shaky. He was nervous to show his vulnerabilities. Such a dominant male thing to do. "How did you figure it out? I was going to tell you, just not until we were further in."

I huffed and wiped my nose, turning away from him. "Jordan and Yolanda decided to wait to mate until his assignment was done. She didn't know that I didn't know."

Eric laid his head back on his head rest, staring at the roof of the car. "He mentioned something earlier about talking to Turner about a replacement for next semester. I'm gonna miss him." His head turned to look at me again. "Cassie, I won't lie to you. I was feeling the pressure to find a mate, but that's not why I want you. I haven't thought about my timeline since the moment I laid eyes on you. Not since you threatened to give my wolf a salad." Eric smiled.

"That was barely 24 hours ago." I pointed out.

He grazed his knuckles down my cheek. "I don't care if it was 24 days ago."

Awe. I lifted a finger and curled it in, telling him to come here. He didn't wait, he didn't hesitate. Eric was mine, as long as I wanted him.

Over the next few months, I saw Eric every day. The four of us met for every lunch, almost every dinner, and we ran every Saturday.

Yolanda started to let her roots grow out, the tawny brown showing. I laughed when Jordan showed up at our dorm room one day with a box of dark blue hair color. Yolanda cried and hugged him. He was supporting her ways and loved her the way she was. A perfect mate for my best friend.

Eric and I were growing closer and closer together. Still, he honored my wishes and did not move things too fast. It made me feel better that he wasn't just with me because he needed a mate.

My wolf and I were both certain that he was someone we could be happy with.

When Thanksgiving came, he dropped me off at the airport before driving home to be with his own family. I had yet to tell mine about Eric.

I sat in the waiting area for my gate, going through pictures of us on my phone. Some were at the lake on Labor Day. We all packed bathing suits into a bag. Jordan carried it to the lake for us, with his wolf teeth. We had a lot of fun that day.

My parents were happily waiting on the other side of the security gate when I walked out. They attacked me at the same time. I was really happy to see my family again. Despite the handsome distraction known as Eric, I had still missed them.

At dinner that night, I pulled out my phone and handed it to my mom. She took a look at the picture of Eric and I and gasped. I giggled. My dad reached for the phone as my mom pulled me into a hug and squealed.

"Whose this?" Pat barked over my dad's shoulder, having gotten up to see it himself.

"That would be Eric."

"And who is Eric exactly?"

I knew what Pat wanted to know. I grinned at him, and his grimace softened. "He may very well be my chosen mate."

Mom, the stronger one in the family, had tears flowing down her eyes.

"What pack is he from?" My dad asked, clearing his throat. Pat sat back down, a frown on his face.

"Eric is the oldest son of Alpha Charles from the Glacier pack, on the borders of Oregon and Washington."

"An Alpha?" Pat seemed a little taken aback by this turn of events.

Our family wasn't typically related to Alphas. Which never bothered us. We were all happy being regular pack members. Well, and pack doctors.

"Yes. He'll be 25 next year." I added softly.

Pat opened his mouth to say more, but mom cut him off. I spent the rest of dinner telling them all about Eric, Jordan, and Yolanda. Pat was quiet throughout the rest of the evening. I both wanted to know what his problem was, and yet, I didn't. I settled for the latter.

I enjoyed my time with my family, it was so good to be with them again. I also knew that my time with them was running short. I needed to soak up all I could of my time with them. If I did officially choose Eric, I would be moving even further away. Permanently. I never imagined myself as a Luna, I still had a hard time picturing it, but if that was what it took to be with Eric, then so be it.

Pat was still distant, much the way he had been over the five days I was home, when they took me to the airport for my return trip on Sunday. It wasn't until he was hugging me goodbye that he finally broke his silence.

He whispered it in my ear, just for me to hear. "I'm here if you need me. Call me if you need to talk about anything. Promise you won't make any rash decisions, Cas?"

I pulled back and looked into his eyes. He was serious. He was seriously worried for some reason. I had no idea why. Eric was a good wolf. He would make a good mate.

"You're the only sister I have left, little one. I can't lose you too."

Awe, butthead. I was doing so good at not crying too. "You won't lose me, Pat. You'll just gain a brother finally."

He shook his head solemnly. "Promise me."

I groaned. "Of course, I won't rush anything." He lifted an eyebrow, forcing me to roll mine in annoyance. "Fine, I promise to not do anything rash. Happy now?"

He smiled and kissed my forehead. "Not quite, but it helps."

CHAPTER 7

Eric

The week away from Cassie was the longest week of my life. We had never even gone a whole day without seeing each other before. It was too much time without her killer smile, her scent, the feel of her in my arms where she belonged.

Mom asked so many questions about her, I was wishing I had brought her home with me, or at least had a copy of all those pictures she had taken of us. Why didn't I? Right, because I was a moron.

Next break, I would bring her home with me. At least for a few days. She could fly to Alaska just as easily from here.

I left home earlier than I normally would have, since I promised to pick her up from the airport. I found it a bit ironic that her flight was shorter than my drive. I parked the car at the airport and half ran to baggage claim, where all the passengers would be coming out. I bounced on my feet, anxious for her to come down that escalator.

I didn't think I had ever missed someone as much as I had missed her this last week.

My movements froze when she began her descent. She was almost more beautiful than I remembered. Her eyes sparkled with joy when they met mine. I caught her mid leap when she jumped into my arms.

I ignored the chuckles of the people walking around us.

"I missed you so much!" She said in between kissing me.

"I missed you, too. I love you, Cassie. Please never leave me so long again."

Cassie froze and leaned back in my arms. "What did you say?"

Oops. Was that too soon? I'd been sitting on that for longer than I would have liked, trying not to push her.

I sucked in a breath. "Was that too soon? I won't take it back. I do love you and I've been dying to …"

From the force she used to kiss me and shut me up, I was guessing it wasn't too soon. She pulled back sooner than I would have liked though. Giggling.

"I love you too, Eric."

I exhaled my relief loudly, causing her to laugh more as she dropped her feet back to the ground. "Let's grab your bag and get out of here."

She lifted a small duffle with one hand and winked at me. "I already have it. It wasn't a long trip and I still have most of my heavy winter clothes at home. I don't exactly need them down here."

I kissed her one more time before taking her bag in one hand and folding her other hand with mine before pulling her out of that airport. She laughed at me the whole way.

I threw her bag in the back seat and pushed her against the side of the car. Cassie didn't seem to mind. Not in the least. At least she didn't, until I got carried away and let my hand slide up further than she had ever allowed before.

In my defense, I wasn't used to females saying no to me. The last three months had felt like an eternity. My wolf and I both wanted to claim her as ours right then. We both loved her, she just said she loved me. So, I relinquished some of my control.

Cassie gasped in a very adorable way, I took it for encouragement, which it apparently was not. Like I said, I didn't usually get turned away. It was new ground for me.

"Eric, stop. We have to stop."

I may have acted like a spoiled two-year-old who did not want to stop playing with his favorite toy. I kissed down her neck and nibbled on the sweet spot that I was dying to bite soon, held her tighter, and pressed my hips into her at the same time.

Her breath was uneven, and I could smell that she wanted this. My wolf pushed his way forward, wanting to check and see if she was ready. We both did. I knew she would love it when we did too. We just had to get her to the point where she wouldn't be able to argue anymore.

"Eric, please? You promised. This is too soon. I'm not ready."

I slowly released my hold and let my head fall onto her shoulders.

"I'm sorry." Cassie was on the verge of crying, which felt like a knife had been shoved through my heart. Automatically making me feel guilty for trying to push my will onto her.

"Don't be sorry, love. I am the one who is sorry. You asked me to stop, and I didn't. I got carried away. We both did." My wolf grumbled in my chest, not wanting to admit that he did too. It was our job to protect our mate, not to hurt her.

Cassie giggled softly. She was still close enough to me, so she probably felt the vibrations of his grumble. She placed one hand over my heart, causing him to sigh.

"Hmmm, I think he likes that." I whispered as I kissed her softly one more time before helping her into the car.

I took her home, carrying her bag all the way up to her room. I sat on her bed and pulled her onto my lap. I was nowhere near ready to go anywhere without her yet.

We were soon joined by Jordan and Yolanda, who had also just returned. From the flush on her cheeks, and the scent in the air, I knew I wasn't the only one struggling to hold back.

I felt bad that I was the reason they couldn't officially mate. It said a lot about Jordan's character and strength that he was holding off until arrangements for his replacement could be made.

My father spoke to Turner the other day. They had another warrior ready, they just had to wait for the new semester to begin. Jordan and Yolanda would be getting a place of their own nearby, at least until they both finished school.

We decided to go to dinner and a movie together. Cassie was going to be working nearly every day for the next week, making up for her absence over the holiday, so we wouldn't get to do much together for a while.

I told her she didn't have to keep working there. Her parents gave her enough money every month and I was willing to give her more if needed. She outright refused. She said the job wasn't about money, it was about being around people and enjoying it. I didn't agree with her decision. But that was mostly because it gave me less time with her. Next semester was going to be even harder. She was already set up to volunteer at the University hospital, which her work schedule would work around. I was never going to see her then.

While we watched the movie, I held her hand tight in mine. I didn't actually *see* any of the movie, I couldn't even remember what the name of it was, or even the genre. Instead. I was making plans to make her mine. Starting with a trip to a certain type of store to get her a special gift for Christmas. Yolanda had been more than happy to measure Cassie's finger while she slept. She did insist that it wasn't for me, it was for Cassie. I didn't care who she did it for, as long as I got the right size.

My dad helped by giving me the number to call Cassie's dad. Alphas had the numbers for all the packs, and her Alpha was more than happy to help. She did say he had chosen his mate as well, so he knew what I was doing.

Things had to be handled differently for chosen than they did for fated mates.

Being in the public eye as a leader of a community, we had to make sure that our matings were also legally bound marriages. Not something every mated couple worried about. It wasn't like divorces happened in shifter communities. but humans had weird expectations of their leaders.

As Cas was my choice, and not my fated, it was important to make sure we had all of our bases covered.

One Friday night, I picked her up from work and took her back to my place, where Yolanda and Jordan were waiting. We had a Netflix and chill night. While I would have preferred to take her to a party - which we had done a few times before - Jordan convinced me that she would have been too tired. He was right. She didn't even make it halfway through the movie. Considering it was my lap she fell asleep on I wasn't complaining anymore.

Once the movie was over, Jordan moved his sleeping mate to his bed, and I took Cassie to mine. Which probably wasn't the best idea. My wolf was going to be grumpy all night and most likely the next morning as well.

We were going to have the mate we had chosen in our bed all night long and I was still refusing to claim her.

She needs to choose us first. We can't force her. You know that.

She wants to, she just needs to get out of her own head. Just like the first time we kissed her. Cassie just needs a little help taking the first step sometimes.

I sighed and fell asleep, holding Cassie in my arms for the first, and only time, as I slept.

I spoke to Cassie's dad the next day. He said he would give us his blessing, as long as it was what Cassie wanted. He also made me promise to take care of her. I had no problems with any of that.

My next call was to our pack doctor and asked about their internship programs for next year. I only told him that a friend of mine was finishing up pre-med and was deciding where to go. I didn't want gossip around the pack to get started just yet. If it did, the whole pack would be sitting in my driveway when we got there. Cassie would absolutely hate that.

When Winter break finally rolled around I was itching to get her home. I was so excited that I was an hour early picking Cassie up from her dorm room. She laughed wholeheartedly when she saw me. I swallowed deeply when I took her in.

Cassie was wearing the world's smallest shorts and a tank top that barely covered her.

"Are you that homesick?" She laughed.

Her smile wasn't helping my growing predicament.

"Pshh, no. I just can't wait to have my family meet you." She yelped with the speed I pulled her to me. "I can't wait to show off this wonderful female I met, who managed to put a spell on me."

Cassie laughed and kissed me, then shoved me away. I always forgot how strong she was. I needed to remember to talk to Ricky about having the females train as well. It wasn't something done in our pack. I liked the idea of them being able to protect themselves if we weren't there though. I wouldn't worry as much when I couldn't be around my mate and pups if I knew they could protect themselves.

Hmm. I couldn't wait to see her stomach round with my pups. I hoped they looked just like her.

"Make yourself comfortable, I'm not ready yet." Cassie patted my chest and started to walk away from me.

Yeah, that wasn't going to fly right now. She squealed and laughed when I threw her over my shoulder and dropped her on the bed, laying down right behind her.

"Not exactly what I meant, babe, and you know it."

I shrugged, not caring. "You said to get comfortable. This is my comfy spot." I pulled her tight against my chest and leaned down to kiss her neck. I heard the small whimper come from her, which made me smile.

By the end of this trip, Cassandra Goodall was going to be my mate. One way or another, we were mating before we came back.

I slid my hand under her shirt and began slowly sliding it up, all the while distracting her with soft kisses on her neck. Yolanda and Jordan left last night since he was going home with her for a bit. So, I knew no one would be coming in to distract her.

"Eric." Her voice was whisper soft, easy enough to pretend I didn't hear her.

"I love you so much, Cassie." I whispered into her neck.

She needed to focus on that fact. We were in love. What else mattered? Nothing, that's what.

She whimpered again, not stopping my hand. I discovered the fun way that she was not wearing a bra yet. Her head fell back against my shoulder when I made it to where I wanted.

She's ready, she wants us. Can't you smell it? Let me check her, Eric. We don't need to wait.

I tried ignoring my inner wolf, but he was making some really good arguments. I continued for another minute. She still wasn't stopping me. She was laying far enough on my right arm that I was able to dip my hand down the top of her shirt, taking over for my left hand, not letting her lose the zen she had found. Then slowly slid the now free one down south, giving her time to stop me.

I didn't go under the waistband. I knew she was distracted enough that there was a good chance I would have gotten away with it, but she would have been mad at me later. I didn't let the barrier bother me though. I still slid my hand far enough down that I reached my goal.

A shiver went through Cassie's body, one I wanted to repeat time and again. I could feel the heat coming from under her shorts, the feeling matched the smell in the room. I didn't know if she was even aware of lifting her upper leg and draping it behind mine. It was enough of an invitation, and the shorts were small enough that they practically opened for more.

I waited a moment longer, long enough for her to whimper and her hips to move against my hand. Apparently she wasn't going to stop me, maybe she was finally ready for us to take the next step, so I gently grazed my hand up her bare thigh and dove in.

See, she just needs our help getting started. We are the Alpha. She will follow our lead.

CHAPTER 8

Cassie

What are you doing, Cassie? Why aren't you stopping him?

I was confused with my wolf. I would have thought she would have been begging for me to let him touch us like this. He had barely gone up my shirt when she started complaining.

Why don't you want to? We've chosen him. I thought you agreed with me?

I did, but you also asked him to stop, and he ignored you.

I didn't really want him to though, and now I really don't want him too.

Cas, you are letting your hormones control you.

Yeah, don't c... care right now. Oh, that... that's new.

You need to stop him, Cassandra.

I whimpered knowing she was right. I meant to move my hand to stop his from doing those wonderful things, but it was my leg that moved instead. Not what I was going for but still not complaining.

Remember your promise to Pat. How many times this month has Eric tried to push things?

He loves us. It's hard to hold back when you love someone.

Shouldn't it be easier to give them what they want when you love them?

Yes, and I love him. I'll stop him soon. Oh, hello.

Stop him now, Cassie!

She didn't wait for me, she pushed forward just enough to make me shoot out of the bed like it was fire and not his hand reaching a whole new danger zone down there.

"Cassie?" Eric sat up, his hand that was obsessively holding me just moments ago, raised out to reach for me.

I straightened my shirt, it was all sorts of weird, then twisted my shorts back to where they belonged.

"Um, yeah. I'm going to go jump in the shower real quick. I'll be ready to leave in about 20. Okay? Okay. Yeah." I turned in a circle, still not sure what I was looking for.

On the desk, Cas. My wolf chuckled at me.

Shut up. I grabbed my bag of clothes and shower supplies off my desk, still a little flustered.

"Cas?" Eric stood up and grasped my arm.

I pulled away and practically ran out the door.

His face was contorted in an odd way when I closed the door behind me. I stood under the cold water longer than normal, trying to cool my libido down. We still had a four-hour drive before getting to his parents' house.

By the time I was dressed and ready to go back to the room, I was feeling self-conscious and embarrassed over the way I reacted.

Should he have stopped long ago? Yes.

Should I have tried harder to stop him? Also, yes.

It was a team failure here. We both made mistakes this morning.

I walked back inside my room, leaning against the closed door, trying to hide the blush when I saw him stretched out on my bed again. Eric smoothly jumped to his feet, stalking slowly to me.

He was being cautious, as though I were a baby rabbit he was trying to catch.

I stayed right where I was, my eyes on my feet. When he was close enough, he lifted my chin up.

"I'm sorry I freaked like that and ran." I whispered.

He huffed out a small laugh. "I'm sorry I keep pushing the line." He flattened his palm to cup my cheek. "I love you, Cassandra. I lose all brain function when I'm with you."

I glanced quickly down. "Well, maybe the right brain does." I teased him with a small laugh.

He laughed too and pulled me against his chest, holding me close. "Yes, the lower brain does seem to take over frequently when it comes to you. The rest of me just goes along for the ride."

I sighed and melted into his chest. "I'm sure it will be a good ride, too. I'm just not there yet, Eric. It's too soon."

I couldn't see his face, but I could hear the pout in his voice. "I know."

Eric's hands had been rubbing my back, but with a flash they were both under my butt and lifting me up. I screeched in a very unladylike fashion as my back hit the wall. I wrapped my legs around his waist, trying not to fall.

Eric looked down, noticing how the skirt I had chosen to wear, wanting to make a good impression on his parents, was now pushed up around my thighs. He licked his lips slowly as his eyes traveled all the way back up to my face.

"Eric." I scolded, albeit a bit breathlessly. Which probably didn't help my case any. "We literally just talked about this."

When his eyes met mine, I noticed they were nearly flat black. His wolf had taken over.

Okay, new ball game here. I knew his wolf had been fighting him, pushing for this. Alpha wolves didn't like waiting to claim their mates. They wanted to mark what they deemed theirs, so no one else would touch it.

I felt my wolf coming forward, ready to teach him a lesson on manners. I wasn't so sure that would go over well for us or the future we were planning.

Let me try first, if I can't calm him down, then I will let you have your way. I pleaded with her.

Her only answer was to back off, but only slightly.

Trusting that he was not about to drop me, I released the death grip I had on his arms and placed both hands on his cheeks. I felt the rumble and the shiver that passed through him. I also saw his teeth lengthening.

I smiled softly, laying my forehead against his.

"Hey, big guy. It's nice to see you."

Eric's wolf gave me a low growl and pressed his lower self into me more. I failed at swallowing the whimpered moan that gave away my need. His claws gripped my waist tighter as he moved against me. His fingers and nails were beginning to lengthen and dig into me.

Oh holy... need to stop.

Don't want to stop.

Need to stop, though. Eric would hate himself if I didn't.

I softly kissed him. "You love us, don't you? You would never hurt us?"

A small pitiful whimper, followed by a voice a lot rougher than Eric's usually was, growled out "Mine!"

I wanted to argue with him, we didn't belong to anybody yet. But there was an extra layer of power in there I had never heard from Eric before, one that made me want to do what he said.

It was his Alpha power.

He was trying to Alpha command me to mate.

It creeped me out and ticked me off all at the same time. Which helped clear my head immediately.

I was trying to figure out another way to calm him down when I felt my consciousness be pushed to the back.

Lovely, now look at what you've done.

"No." My wolf growled, dropping our legs, and shoving him back further than I ever could have.

Eric's wolf growled deeply in a chuckle, enjoying the challenge. It was possible he thought she was going to make him chase her. The domination game, all part of mating. When he stalked closer, a hunter after his prey, she lifted a foot and kicked him in the chest, pushing him all the way across the room.

Holy, fur balls. You go, girl! I cheered her on.

"Not until we say so. You try that Alpha power crap with us again and you can forget about it. You want us as your mate, then you better prove you will honor us and respect us. We are not here for you to push around. That's not what a mate does! That's not what the Alpha power is for. You are better than this."

Eric's eyes closed, and he shook his head, from his crouched position on the floor. I could hear a small whimpering coming from within him. My wolf retained control, taking us further away from them, our arms folded across our chest. We watched as Eric's body shivered, those few seconds lasted an hour.

When he stood up again, his eyes were back to their normal light brown color. Mine, on the other hand, I knew were still glowing a bright silver, as they did when my wolf took over.

Eric raised an apologetic hand, waiting for me to take it. I would have, but my wolf was more stubborn than I was.

"I'm sorry, he's sorry. We both are. We lost control. He promises to not use the Alpha tone again."

Oh, that's what that was. I wasn't completely sure. It felt weird. Is that why you came out?

She huffed at me. *Obviously. He was beyond what you were capable of handling. I'm not sure I trust that he won't try it again.*

Give it time.

We'll see.

With that, she faded into the background again.

"Well, this has been an eventful morning. Are you ready to go?" I gave him that can we please just move on now grin.

Eric laughed and picked up my bag, before coming to me. "I'm sorry, Cas. I never should have picked you up like that, especially in a skirt. I knew he was getting impatient, I just didn't…"

I put my hand over his lips. "I know. We just need to be extra careful from now on." He was being so sweet about everything. It made it really hard to be mad at him. For me anyway. Wolves weren't as easy to convince though. She just huffed in my head again.

He took my hand off his lips and held it in his. "That right there, your heart, is one of the many reasons why I love you, Cassandra Goodall. I really want to kiss you again." He kissed me on the back of the hand he still held. "But I think this may be all we can handle for right now."

I smirked and folded my fingers with his. Without another word, we left for the long, and slightly awkward, drive to meet his family.

CHAPTER 9

Cassie

The ride to Vancouver was eerily quiet. Usually when we were in the car, Eric would be holding my hand or resting his on my knee. Not this time. This time, he kept his distance from me. I knew why he was doing it, but it still hurt.

We tried talking on and off, but no conversation stuck. That was how we spent the first two hours of our drive.

I nearly jumped out of my skin when Eric exhaled loudly, like a big battle was over. His hand automatically reached for mine, holding it tight. He even kissed it.

"Sorry, sweetheart."

"Have you two been talking this entire time?" It was the only thing I could think of.

Eric gave a small, shy smile. "Yes. He really does promise to not use his Alpha authority on you like that again. We had to have a talk on why he can't force you to be ready that way. He seems to think we just need to push you out of your head."

I frowned at him. Eric laughed softly and kissed my hand again. "I explained to him why that would be worse for us in the long run. Like you said, we just need to watch what we do for a while." He winked at me, making me think he had some type of secret.

I had long suspected that Eric was planning on officially asking me to be his mate. If he had asked before this morning, I would have said yes without a doubt in my mind. We often talked about chosen mates since I found out he was an Alpha.

I knew he loved me, but that didn't mean that he wouldn't drop me like a fly if his fated walked by.

After this morning though, I was a little worried. Was he just dragging things along until he got what he wanted? Did he really love me? Or was he just trying to say all the right things until I gave in? Was that what Pat was worried about?

My wolf was right, if Eric did love me as much as he said he did, he wouldn't keep pushing me like he had been. And neither would his wolf. Did Eric know there was a difference between love and lust?

I sighed quietly to myself, laying my head down on his shoulder and holding his arm. Eric moved his hand to my knee, holding me while I was holding him. This was something we had done many times on our way on and off the mountain, after our Saturday runs. I used to find comfort in it, now I wasn't so sure. I was constantly on guard for his hand to move to places it didn't belong. It wasn't like it would be the first time he "teased" me by doing that.

We were silent for another half hour, left to our own thoughts, before he spoke again. "I... uh. Have a confession to make."

I sat up and lifted an eyebrow. What now?

"I arranged a time for you to meet with our pack doctor." He looked at me quickly, probably gauging my reaction, before turning back to the road.

I waited for him to continue before reacting.

"I know I should have talked to you first, asked what you wanted. I just got really excited by the idea and wanted all the information before I came to you."

"Stop rambling out excuses and tell me what you did." I managed to keep my voice steady, not giving away any emotions. It was still a toss-up of where he was going with this.

He cleared his throat, knowing me well enough to know he better speak fast, and chuckled softly.

"I was hoping that next year you could transfer to the university down here and do your internship at our hospital. Dr. Shapiro agreed to meet with you and let you tour our hospital."

I swallowed the little girl squeal. He was planning for us to still be together next year. I mean, talking about it was one thing, planning it was another.

Yes, but we haven't decided if we even want to go that route yet. He knows that.

He's giving us options. He doesn't want to stand in the way of what we do want. It's not like he already had my credits transferred and confirmed me going there. It's just a tour of the hospital and a meeting with the doctor I could be working with. It would be better to learn from a pack doctor than a human one.

My wolf gave me an aggrieved sigh.

Why are you not happy with the mate we had both chosen? Have you changed your mind?

Yes and no. I'm not happy with the way things have been lately. He's trying too hard. Harder than he used too.

He wants us to be happy. This is what you do for those that you love.

Not exactly, Cas. You also have to let them live their own lives and make their own decisions. He isn't happy when we make decisions that don't include him. I agree he is trying. But something isn't sitting right.

Are you changing your mind?

Not yet. Just on the fence.

"Cas?"

I looked up at Eric, the worried expression was back. "Are you mad at me for not talking to you first? Is she?"

I gave one soft ha! "She's not happy that you keep pushing for things that you think we want, without talking to us. I know you are just trying to help, Eric, but I haven't decided if I want to continue with medical school. I don't know if I even want to do an internship."

His hand squeezed my leg. "I know. I just wanted you to know that you have options. I just… I don't want you to feel like you have to choose between me and your career. I want a future with you, Cas. I want you."

I sucked in some air, shocked at where this conversation had gone. This was more definite sounding than he had been in the past.

"I haven't talked about the future with you because I wanted you to have the time you needed to decide what you want. I love you, Cas. I know I've made mistakes, but I am trying to do better. I will always try to do better for you."

I felt the blush warming my cheeks. "I wasn't sure you still wanted more. You hadn't said anything."

"What? Babe, I told you I love you."

I shrugged, nonverbally telling him that wasn't always enough.

He nodded, understanding my meaning. "I'm going to make up for that. I will make sure you always know that you are the one I chose, not the one I was forced to have, the one I chose to have."

From the beginning, I'd known he didn't care about fated mates. I never realized just how much he didn't like it though. Part of me was honored with the idea that he chose me, but another small part was upset. I wasn't sure why.

"What happened that turned you against fated mates so much, Eric?"

He gave a one shoulder shrug. "Nothing really. I know a lot of wolves that found their fated mates and are perfectly happy. Nearly every one of them had to uproot their lives though. One of the mates always had to leave something they loved behind, they had to make a choice."

"Yeah, but all mates are like that, even chosen ones. If I choose you..." he turned and raised an eyebrow at me. So, I said it again, with emphasis. "*If* I choose you…" I squealed when he pinched the inside of my leg.

After a minute of giggles, I finally finished. "I would still have to leave my family behind, Eric. That's how it is with everyone, even the humans."

"That part is true, I guess. But at least we have time, we are not completely floored with the fate bond, making it so we cannot even think straight."

"Says the man who could hardly string two words together when we met and lost control over his wolf just this morning." I kept my voice and face deadpan.

He grimaced and I lost it. He pinched me again.

"We do have one fated pair in our pack that never should have happened. They met at a party, celebrating finishing high school, about two years ago. She came from the neighboring pack. She comes from a really nice family. He is a douche. Always has been, always will be.

He convinced her to move down here with him a week after they met. The pack helped build them a little house near his parents. I've always wondered if she would have changed her mind had she had more time to get to know him. Or if he would have been different if he actually had to work for it."

"What happened?"

"They're still there. He's the pack drunkard and she is his punching bag."

"That's so sad. But, Eric, that's a more recent circumstance. I'm sure you've felt like this for a while."

He nodded slowly. "True. I have. It's just confirmation for me that fated mates aren't always the best choice. I don't really know when it started. Maybe it has something to do with Ricky."

"Your brother? I thought you said he hadn't met his mate yet?"

Eric gave a small smile, the same one he always had when he thought of his brother.

"Nah. But even before his first shift, he was always adamant about waiting for his mate. He never dated anyone in school. He always said there was no point. He was waiting for his mate. He went stag to prom and danced with everyone. None of the males cared, they all knew how Ricky was. But he has put off possibly finding something awesome." He gripped my leg tighter, making me swoon just a bit. "For something that may never happen."

"So, since he went the extreme one way, you went the other?"

Eric huffed a few laughs. "Yeah, I guess I did. That seems to be us in a nutshell, going in two different directions. I can't wait for you to meet him. Honestly, Ricky should have been born first. I have no problem admitting it. He is the more mature one out of the two of us. The more stable and down to earth, maybe even the more reliable."

"You are all those things too. Don't cut yourself short. It's easier to see the good in others than it is to see in ourselves."

Eric leaned over and kissed my cheek quickly. "I love you, Cas."

I turned my head and kissed his shoulder, then placed my chin on it to look at him. "I love you, too."

For the last hour of our long drive, we talked about all the places he wanted to take me to in his hometown and the people he wanted me to meet. I had a feeling it was going to be a very busy week.

That was all I had promised him, one week.

I was leaving the day after Christmas to go back to Alaska. I had been thinking about taking him with me, but I just couldn't bring myself to ask him. I didn't know why. The way Eric was talking though, the one week was going to be longer than seven days. A few minutes ago, the idea that he wanted to keep me thrilled me. The more he talked though, the less excited I was.

Maybe it was because, once again, he was doing all the planning. It was his home though, and my first time there. So, I let it go. He was excited to have me there with him, that was all.

CHAPTER 10

Ricky

"Morning, mom." I gave her a quick kiss as I passed her in the kitchen.

"Morning, Ricky." She smiled at me. When she noticed my outfit though, it slipped faster than a mudslide. "Why are you wearing your uniform? You said you were getting today off so we could all meet Cassie together." She turned to fully face me as she spoke, one hand moving to rest on her hip, her opposite foot tapping on the floor.

"I did have today off. Unfortunately, Gamma Allen called me a few minutes ago. Officer Chris can't go in today." I grinned, knowing the next part would make the pack Luna happy. "His mate went into labor last night. Her water broke around five am. She's still in labor and he doesn't want to leave her."

She squealed and clapped her hands, proving me right..

"Oh, I am so happy for them. I guess that's a good enough reason for you having to work. You can meet Cassie tomorrow."

I laughed as my mom took a deep breath and shook out her arms. I gave her a quick hug.

"Don't be so nervous, mom. Everything is going to go perfectly. You have the guest room made up, you have extra everything in there for her. You even have dinner planned out for just the family tonight."

She nodded, not really listening to me. "This is a big deal, Ricky. We both know how hard it was for your brother to pick someone." She wiped a tear from under her eye. "I always assumed he would eventually find his fated mate, but I should have known better. That boy is filled with pure stubbornness. He always had to have things his way."

I shook my head and laughed lightly. Ain't that the truth, and that was stating it mildly. Eric never did take hearing the word "no" very well. I had no proof of course, but I was fairly certain he used the Alpha tone a time or two to get away with being late for school on occasion.

"From what he says, she puts him in his place, mom. That's exactly what he needs."

She nodded again and rubbed her thumb on my cheek. "True. Now we just need you to go on vacation or something. We need to help you find your mate. Maybe you can go visit Gamma's in other packs."

I sighed, not in the mood for this conversation again. It didn't matter how many times I told them; my wolf insisted we stay here. Our mate was going to come to us. We didn't know how or why, just that she would.

I kissed my mother's cheek one more time and headed for the door. "I need to go. I will probably be home late. So, I will see you in the morning." I stopped and looked at her sternly, one finger pointing at her. "Don't scare her off, female."

Mom gasped and I winked at her. Something hit the wall behind me as I took off out the door, laughing.

I gave myself a minute to think while I was still locked in my cruiser, sitting outside the station.

I loved my brother, but I was envious. Sometimes I wished I could be more like him and just choose someone. That wasn't for me though. My wolf and I had no doubts that we would find our mate. The one who was perfect for us in every way. Someone I wouldn't have to explain why I chose to do the things I did to or adjust to their personalities. My mate was going to be just right, for both my wolf and me. She would get us. Get the fact that I was laid back. Get the fact that I wanted to protect my pack and wasn't in it for the glory. She'd liven me up a bit once in a while, but otherwise, love me for who I was. Not who she could make me be.

And I would love her just the same. I wouldn't mind going out to places with her every now and then, take her for a night on the town. It would be worth it, just to see my mate smile. If she needed me to hide her and protect her from the world, I could do that too.

I pushed the thoughts out of my head as I walked into the station. I sat down and got started on the pile of paperwork sitting on my desk.

Reports that needed to be written.

Reports that needed to be filed.

Reports that needed to be edited and sent back to the deputy who wrote it, to redo it.

I hated paperwork. I didn't join the force to do paperwork. Just the word itself felt like a dirty word on my lips, leaving a bad aftertaste in my mouth.

After three hours of nonstop paperwork, I wanted a drink, and I didn't drink. Ever. I'd seen too many people, humans, and wolves alike, who let the drink get the better of them.

Days like this were prime examples of why I didn't actually want to be Gamma. It was my duty though. It was what Eric wanted. Allen Jr. got to follow his mate to her pack. Which meant, his responsibility fell to me.

Most days I didn't mind so much. I loved my pack. They were my family. I wanted to protect them. Besides, I could always relegate the paperwork to someone else to do. Maybe hire an actual secretary for the station.

Yeah, that would be great. I should definitely do that.

Gamma Allen Sr. came in a little later. We talked for a bit. His first grandbaby was now on the way. Seemed like everyone was moving on but us.

Will you stop with the whining today? Man, you are in a mood. My wolf griped at me.

Shut up. You're just as frustrated as I am. And for the record, your incessant pacing in there isn't helping.

I can't help it. My wolf snapped back. *Something's coming, something big.*

Any ideas on what it is?

No, I can just feel it in the air.

Okay, we'll keep an eye out.

The day was long. We spent more time with human problems than we did with wolf problems. Allen and I traded off with driving around and answering the phone in the station. Around dinner time, we got a call about a domestic disturbance. This one was from the pack side of town.

Allen didn't even need to tell me the address, I already knew.

Ten minutes later I was pulling up outside the small building I helped build just a few years earlier. I grunted as I pulled myself out of my cruiser and headed for the front door. I raised my hand to knock, freezing as I heard a scream and then a loud bang.

It sounded like someone had been thrown against a wall, a wall like the one that just shook next to me. With the help of my wolf, I could smell blood too.

Screw knocking, I now had probable cause.

I pulled my gun out of my belt and opened the door carefully, looking around the room. I spotted Nathan standing over what looked like a lumpy blanket, which had a small stream of blood flowing from it.

"Get out of here, Ricky. This doesn't concern you."

I held my gun on him carefully, watching for the slightest movement from him.

"Everything in this town concerns me, Nate. This pack, especially, is under my protection. I won't let you hurt her."

He finally looked up at me, fire blaring in his eyes. I expected to see his wolf, but it was pure Nate.

"She is my mate. Fate gave her to me. I will treat her the way I see fit. She needs to learn to watch her mouth."

I stepped closer, waving him back with my gun. At least he was smart enough to step further back. Many members of the pack blamed Nate's wolf, saying he was borderline feral. I was of a different opinion. One my father was beginning to believe.

I knew Nate in school, my wolf and I always felt like his wolf was more submissive than the human side. Nate, the human side, was prone to bouts of anger, hungry for some measure of power. His wolf on the other hand was submissive, he didn't care about power. I believed that ticked Nate off even more.

In fact, I was pretty sure his mate's wolf was more dominant than his. Which could be why he was always quick to bring her down. I'd be proud to have a mate that was more dominant than me. It meant fate thought I was deserving of such a female.

I made it to Allie, and slowly bent down, keeping my gun and eyes on Nate. With my other hand, I reached down and checked for a pulse. I gave her one quick glance before standing back up again. I didn't need to say anything to her, she was out cold. I was sure her wolf was listening though and knew I was there. I hoped she would take comfort in my presence, knowing I would get them the help they needed.

I pulled my radio off my belt and pushed down the button. "Gamma, we need an ambulance for Allie."

He didn't need to push the button down for me to hear him. I could imagine him cursing like a sailor just fine.

"Roger that, they are on the way."

"Thanks, I'll be back soon with Nate."

"Got it, over and out."

I carefully placed my radio back on my belt and pulled out my cuffs. I signaled with my finger for him to turn around.

He growled but did as he was told. I was larger and ten times more dominant than him. Something he no doubt hated.

"She's fine, she'll sleep it off and then tell you all that it was a misunderstanding. Just like she does every other time you butt your heads into our business."

I grabbed his arms and pulled them behind him, locking the cuffs around his wrists. I lost count of how many times we had been through this.

"Not this time, Nate. I'm going to have the Alpha release her and send her back to her own pack."

Nate snarled and started pulling away, but it was too late. I had him cuffed and a firm grasp on his arm.

"She's my mate! You can't take her away from me. I will get her back!"

"Not this time, bud. My father can dissolve a bond. He doesn't like to do it, but he can."

Nate snarled again. "He can't do that. It takes two Alpha's to dissolve a bond. By the time you get another one here, she will have come back to me."

I patted his shoulder sadly as I led him out the front door, the ambulance pulling up as we walked down the two steps.

"It's your lucky day. Eric is back in town for the holidays. He carries an Alpha wolf. Between the two of them, they should have enough power to dissolve your bond."

I dipped his head and pushed him inside the back of my cruiser before going back inside to check on Allie.

I was at the party when she and her friends showed up. Just like every other time we got visitors, I held out a shred of hope that one of them was mine. I'd never seen Nate so quiet as the moment he saw her.

Our mates were supposed to be able to calm us, to balance us. Somewhere, something went wrong.

They were good together for the first few weeks. I guess he just couldn't handle her being more dominant than him. He made the choice and ruined it for both of them. It wasn't too late though. She could still find a chosen one down the road.

When she was ready to trust a male again. She wouldn't be the first female to turn to a human after a fated pairing went wrong. Of course, in those instances, it was usually because the mate's wolf went feral. And the surviving mate needed someone more docile. The fear of another feral mate wasn't easy to get over.

I waited while the paramedics loaded her up into their ambulance. Allie had a cut across her forehead, she was a lot skinnier than the last time I saw her too. Maybe malnourished. I could see older bruises covering her arms and ribs.

"Why haven't those healed? They look old."

The paramedics, who were thankfully of the shifter variety, looked them over. One of them looked back at the house.

"I suggest you search for wolfsbane. He may have been feeding it to her so she couldn't heal or fight back."

I swore. "Yeah. I'll do just that. Thank you."

I went back to my cruiser, needing to take care of my cargo first. Nate yelled, cursed, and threatened me the whole way back to the station. As we walked through the door, he had to get one more out of his system.

His voice was low and slippery. "Just wait, Ricky. You took my mate. I'm going to take yours from you, show you how it feels.'

I smirked, knowing it would tick him off more. "Don't have one." I shrugged nonchalantly. "Good luck with that."

"I can wait. When you get her, don't get comfortable."

I nodded out of habit, tired of this already. I handed him over to Gamma Allen, our town Sheriff, and explained where I needed to go. He frowned but gave me approval. Half an hour after I left to deliver Nate, I was walking back inside the home that hadn't seen a day of happiness since the day it was created.

I decided to start in the far back bedroom and work my way forward. I hadn't gotten very far when I heard the front door open. I peeked out the bedroom door and saw the two paramedics stepping inside.

"Where do you want us?" The same one from before asked.

I gave them each a pair of plastic gloves, a starting point, and they got to work.

It took the three of us two hours, but we found it. A small bottle of wolfsbane. It had been hidden in plain sight. It was in the cabinet with all the seasonings. It was pushed to the far back, with all the less used seasonings.

On its own, wolfsbane wasn't exactly deadly. Unfortunately, it practically paralyzed our wolves. Making us weaker, almost human. Hence the name, wolfsbane. It was the bane of our wolf's existence.

"Thank you for your help, gentlemen. I'll swing by and let the hospital know, then I have to process this into evidence." I slipped it into an evidence pouch that I kept in my belt, just in case the time came, and I needed one.

Eric still liked to tease me, calling me a boy scout. Nothing wrong with being prepared.

"Any time, Rick. See you later." The quieter one walked out, followed by his partner. Who then froze in the door. "Hey. Eric was due back today, wasn't he?"

I laughed. "Yeah, he should already be back at the pack house. Mom doesn't want anyone around tonight though. Give it a day or two, let her smother him first."

He laughed and walked out. I could have mentioned Cassie, but I knew Eric would rather have the honor of introducing her to the pack. I was not going near that crater of lava. There were going to be some pretty ticked off females in this pack.

My brother left more than one heart weeping when he left. I had to hope Cassie was strong enough to stand her ground when they all came with their torches and pitchforks. Eric and his whole chosen mate bull gave too many of them hope that he would choose them to be his mate and Luna of the pack. Really wasn't his smartest decision. Not that he had ever made many of those anyway.

Plenty of dumb ones that was for sure.

Either way, she was going to get a lot of attention, for the good and the bad. With time running short until he became Alpha, the elders in the pack were antsy. The younger ones were cautious, but not quite to the point of the elders.

Allie was still sleeping when I made it to the hospital. Dr. Shapiro said he sedated her, keeping her in the coma until they could start the healing process. I showed him what we found, he cursed, and gave new orders to the nurses. At least now they knew what they were working with.

By the time I got back to the station, it was well after ten. I logged the poison into evidence. Harassed the night shift deputy for a few minutes and then headed for home. Everyone would be asleep, but that was fine. I just wanted to shower and pass out. I was in no shape to see anyone.

I barely stepped two feet in the front door when my wolf stood at attention. *That smell. Where is the owner of that luscious smell?*

I searched around the downstairs floor of the pack house, but I couldn't find where it was coming from. As I headed up the stairs, the smell lingered. It was spread evenly throughout each floor. No way to know who it had come from.

Mom probably had someone come in and help clean earlier. We can ask her in the morning who it was. You're going to have to calm down though.

My wolf whimpered but was otherwise silent. I took a hot shower, hoping it would soothe my inner beast. I tried laying down, feeling completely exhausted. The mutt wouldn't knock it off though. He kept pacing and mumbling about the smell.

When he got like this, there was only one way to soothe him. I was exhausted, but at least I could hand over the reins to him and chill.

I didn't even bother getting fully dressed again. I only pulled a pair of shorts on, and that was just in case Cassie came out of the room. I did not want to meet my future sister-in-law while wearing only my boxers.

I stripped them off as I hit the patio, letting my beast free. With him physically on the outside, the scent was stronger. With only one word, he took off for the woods.

Mine.

CHAPTER 11

Cassie

My leg was bouncing with nerves by the time we pulled up in front of the pack house. Eric thought it was hilarious. Such a jerk.

He placed a hand on the leg doing a rabbit impression. "Calm down. They are going to love you. Just… not the way I do."

I smirked at his lame attempt at humor. He leaned forward and kissed me softly before getting out of the car.

My legs were frozen, I couldn't move. Not that he was going to give me a choice in the matter. Eric was already at my door, opening it, and then pulling me out against my will. Still laughing. If he kept it up, this leg was going to bounce high enough to hit something he valued. See if he would be able to push me then.

Tempting. He'd deserve it after this morning. But I doubt the Luna would appreciate us emasculating her son in front of her.

 I sighed. *Party pooper.*

My wolf softly chuckled.

We didn't even make it to the front patio before the door was opened. A female, roughly the same age as my mom, came hurrying out. She practically threw her arms around Eric, then started leaving kisses all over his face.

Eric blushed. I enjoyed his embarrassment. It was a perfect example of karma, and exactly what he deserved for laughing at me.

Not as good as kneeing him would have been though.

I laughed at my wolf, since she was the one who had been talking me out of it but didn't comment otherwise.

"Mom, it's barely been a month!"

She kissed his cheek one more time and held his face firmly in her hands. "One month, one day, one year. All the same. Wait until you have pups, let's see how well you handle it."

"As I am a male, I'm betting better than you."

I huffed. "You say that now. My father is worse than my mother." I grimaced and bit my lip. I had broken her trance and now her eyes were pointed at me. Good going, Cas.

Next thing I knew, the pack Luna was squealing and hugging me. "I am so happy to see you!" She grabbed my hand and pulled me in the house.

I laughed as Eric mumbled. "Guess I'll grab our bags then."

She ignored him completely for the next hour as she asked me every question that popped into her head. I couldn't help but laugh at the look on Eric's face. It was a mix of both offended that he had been forgotten about already and proud that his mom was so happy about me being there.

We were sitting in the living room, somewhat comfortable, Eric by my side, when I smelled someone new joining us.

"Female, will you let the young pup have a breath please. You have all week to get to know her. There is no reason to shove it all into a few hours." The voice that floated in was deep and joyful. It was soon followed by an older version of Eric.

The Alpha entered the room and put a hand up for me to shake. I nervously took it and shook his hand. The only Alpha I had ever met was the one for my home pack. And that had never been in any real intimate social situation like this was. It always involved business of some sort, or a pack party where there were at least two hundred other wolves around.

"Welcome, Cassie. In case my mate hasn't made it clear, we are very happy to have you in our home."

I smiled shyly and dipped my head. "Thank you." I felt Eric's hand on my back, rubbing gently. Which helped me breathe a little easier.

Eric looked behind his father. "Where is Ricky?"

"Chris's mate went into labor in the early hours of the morning, Ricky got called in to cover his shift. He'll be home later tonight."

Eric frowned. I felt bad his brother wasn't here, but a new pup was more important than him being here to greet us.

I put a hand on his knee. "We'll have to make sure to send congratulations to the new parents. Is this their first pup?"

Bea, as she insisted I call her because she hated the name Beatrice, nodded with a giant grin. "It is. They tried for so long to get a pup. We were starting to worry it wouldn't happen."

"Well, I'm glad that Chris could be there with her. His mate comes first." I glared at Eric, hoping to get the point across.

He rolled his eyes, but I saw a smile.

When I looked back at his parents, his mom was glowing. Her mate walked around her to sit beside her on the love seat. We talked and got to know each other better, visiting I guess it was called, until dinner time. I insisted on helping Luna Bea get everything ready. She made a simple chicken casserole. Which I loved.

We played a few rounds of cards afterwards, until I started yawning. That seemed to have been the clue that it was time for bed. Eric led me up to the second floor, his parents went up to the third. We went down a hallway and passed two closed doors.

An enticing scent was lingering around one, perking up my wolf's ears. The scent was very faint, but it did smell good.

"This is you." Eric stopped in front of a door across and down a few feet from the last one we passed.

He trapped me between him and the door, standing so close I had to look up or have my nose smashed into his chest.

"Want me to come tuck you in?" His eyes twinkled. He was radiating pure happiness tonight.

I shook my head, smiling and silently laughing as his smile slipped. "Nope. We agreed in the car, we were going to take a step back, remember?"

He pouted and dropped his head to my shoulder. "Dang. I forgot." He kissed my shoulder gently before lifting back up to me and kissing my lips. "If you change your mind, I'm *all* the way at the end of the hall. Right next to the stairs."

I kissed him one more time, feeling oddly awkward about doing it. "Good night, Eric. I'll see you in the morning."

Exhaling with a groan, he pushed off the door, and stepped away slowly, as I walked into my room. My bags were sitting on the bed, where I assumed he dropped them off while his mother played five rounds of 20 questions.

I unpacked my things, feeling grateful their guest room had its own bathroom. The last thing Eric and his wolf needed was to see me in a towel or freshly out of the shower. Once I was settled in, I realized my wolf was anything but.

What's the matter?

That smell.

What about it?

I don't know. I wish it had been stronger. There was something to it.

We can ask Eric about it in the morning.

Fine. I could feel her lay down with a huff. *I still don't trust him. Did you see how upset he got because his brother chose to help someone else today? The birthing of a pup is more important than waiting a few hours to see someone.*

I sighed. *I know. He is learning it isn't all about him. Are you going to let me sleep any time soon?*

No.

I sighed and looked around the room. The stars were beautiful tonight. I wouldn't mind getting a better look.

Wanna run? I asked her like I was trying to tempt her out. I kind of was. I was trying to tempt her out of a bad mood.

Yes, that would be wonderful. We haven't run alone in a while. We could use the time to think properly.

Not what I was going for, but I would take it. I was already down to my shorts and tank that I usually slept in, but with everyone else asleep, it should be fine.

I tiptoed down the hall, trying not to alert Eric that I was leaving. He did not need to see me in this outfit again.

I paused at his door and listened carefully. I swallowed the giggle when I heard the faint traces of a snore. He still swore that he didn't snore, no matter how many times Jordan and I said otherwise.

One day I might just record it for him.

He'd still deny it and claim it was fake.

I giggled softly at my wolf. That was very true.

I continued down the hall, down the stairs, and out what I assumed was the back patio door. I shivered as the cold air hit me, then took off running to the nearest trees, stripped behind one and shifted. It felt like I was stretching a sore muscle.

We ran in peace for a solid half hour before we found a small clearing, with a perfect view of the sky. She knew what I needed, and why I really wanted to run.

Sometime later, I felt my eyes drooping. The moon was high in the sky now.

Are you ready to get back? It's late.

She didn't respond to me. Instead, she lifted her head and looked back at the way we came. I was about to ask her what was wrong, but then I heard it too. The sounds of large paws running toward us.

Do you think Eric realized we were gone?

No, I know the sound of his paws hitting the ground. He is too graceful, too light footed. This is the sound of a warrior on the hunt.

I didn't like the sound of that. *We need to leave. We need to go now. We never should have left the house alone in a strange territory.*

She reacted to my anxiety mentally but did not move. *I don't feel danger coming.* I heard her take a big sniff of the air, and then sigh deeply. *It's that smell again, it's getting stronger.*

We both watched as a large sandy wolf entered the clearing.

CHAPTER 12

Ricky

Slow down. We don't know who is out there. I warned my wolf, who was running like he was on a hunt.

I do. Can't you smell it? Can't you smell her?

Who?

Our mate! Breathe in the scent, Rick. You know it too.

I took a slow deep breath, not easy to do when my wolf was running faster than a race car driving on the highway. His large legs ate up the long distance quickly. I focused on the scent, and it sent tingles throughout my body.

He was right. The smell from the house was all over these woods, he was following the trace of lilacs and cinnamon.

Slow down, you will scare her if we come at her like this.

He grunted but did as I said.

By the time we entered a small clearing, where the smell was the strongest, he was walking again. Right in the middle was a gorgeous silver wolf. I had heard of gray, but I had never heard of silver.

The way the moonlight danced in her fur; she could have been part of it. It was like the moon had laid her right there for us to find. A treasure.

She was lying on her belly, her head turned to watch us enter. As we got closer, she slowly stood on all fours, her eyes on us, and then took off.

I was confused at first, then tuned into my wolf's reaction. He was giddy.

Mine! I will catch our mate and I will prove our worth to her.

She was fast. She covered nearly half a mile before we caught up to her. My wolf hit the gas as he got closer, jumping in front of her, blocking her path. I expected him to come at her from the side and push her over. But that might have hurt her.

Instead, he blocked her and then shoved his head under her's, nuzzling her. I heard the light-hearted humming coming from our mate. Then she pushed us and took a few steps back. She lowered her head, daring us to come forward.

We gave out a low deep throated chuckle. We preened at the way her body shivered at the sound. Then we accepted her dare.

For the next fifteen minutes, we played with our mate. We wrestled with her. Sometimes she got the upper hand, sometimes we did.

We had her pinned below us, in between our large paws. Both of us steadying our breath. Suddenly, I felt a shift in the air. Something changed. Her head turned back and forth, looking around. It was like a spell had been broken. Then just as suddenly she shifted into her human form.

I quickly followed suit.

Her hair glowed brightly in the moonlight, just like her fur did. Her eyes were confused and a little scared. I wondered if she realized that I was her mate. Did she not understand what this meant?

My wolf surged forward, urging me on. *Kiss her, show her who we are to her.*

There was no way I was going to argue with that. I'd been waiting my whole life to do this. The moment our lips met; I felt a shock run through my body. I felt something snapping into place. A hole I didn't even know was there, was now filled.

If I had any lingering doubts about who this female was, they were gone. She was my fated mate. She was meant to be mine. Her reaction told me she felt it too. She melted into me. I could feel her body molding itself around mine.

Claim her, claim her now. Let me check her. She is ours and she can't get away.

That's a bit fast, especially for us. Take it down a couple notches.

I pulled away, just enough to see her beautiful face once more. She was smiling up at me, which lasted for about two heartbeats. Then the panicked look came back.

"No." She whispered. It sounded so sad, yet majestic at the same time.

I was too shocked to understand what was going on as I watched her push away from me, shaking her head, whispering no, over, and over again. She stopped and gave me one last sad look, then shifted and took off.

We need to shift, we need to chase, we need to catch her again.

No. She isn't testing us this time. Something's wrong.

Catch her, ask her. We don't even know her name!

I could hear him howling in my head, begging for our mate to come back. It took all I had to not let him regain control and force the shift. He tried harder than he ever had when he first emerged. When it was normal for pups to still be adjusting to who was in control.

Not yet. Her scent is all over the house. We can ask mom in the morning.

We know everyone in the pack, no one new has come to town. Lovely, he was moping now. He was insufferable when he was mopey.

Maybe Cassie and Eric brought another friend with them.

Hmmm, that is possible, I guess.

I waited there, sitting on the cold ground, freezing my… manhood off. Trying to give her plenty of time to get to wherever she was going. Just in case he changed his mind again.

Her scent was still surrounding the house, just as it had when we left. There was no way to tell how old it was or whether she had been coming or going. Her scent clung to everything. Somehow it had even bled through the crack under my door.

Before I had left, I had opened my window, hoping it would help air out my room.

I was wrong. It was just icy cold to boot.

Which was probably a good thing since neither my wolf, nor I could forget about our beautiful mate. The cold helped keep my own issues from getting worse.

I tossed and turned all night, falling asleep around dawn. Exhaustion had finally taken its toll on my body and forced the rest of me to fall asleep.

At one point, I heard soft voices in the hall. I pulled a pillow over my head and went back to sleep. It didn't last long.

Hey, lazy butt! Get down here so I can see your ugly mug. I got someone I want you to meet.

I let him hear my groan through the link. He let me hear his responding chuckle.

Yes, let's get down there, see if they know who our mate is.

Memories of the night before flooded through my sleep deprived brain. I jumped out of bed feeling like somebody had just poured a gallon of coffee down my gullet. I showered and dressed as quickly as I could.

As soon as I stepped outside my door, I was hit with a fresh trail of her scent.

Yes! She's here! Follow it, hunt her, chase her, claim her!

Alright Romeo, calm down. First we find her, then we figure out why she ran. We will claim her, but you need to be patient. She has to know that we are here for her, not her for us. Think of Nate and Allie.

He grumbled a few choice swear words in regard to Nate. I heavily agreed with him of course.

The trail led us down the stairs and toward the kitchen. I took a deep whiff, letting her scent roll through my body like a drug. The goosebumps spread throughout my body, coating me.

As I came around the corner, out from behind my parents, I heard my brother's voice.

"You alright, sweetheart? Catch a chill?"

An awkward feminine chuckle sounded next, with a small soft voice following. "I'm fine, Eric."

No, no, no. No, no, no. This could not be happening. I paused in the hall when I heard her voice but pushed myself forward.

The second I laid eyes on her she looked up and met mine. The same sad, scared look was there. She then looked over to my older brother, whose arm was wrapped around the back of the chair she sat in.

CHAPTER 13

Ricky

"About time Ricky! How late did you get home last night?"

I cleared my throat and swallowed, praying for a miracle, praying for a misunderstanding.

"Just before eleven, but I went for a run after."

My father turned around to look at me, catching the stress in my voice. I forced my eyes away from her sky-blue eyes, and shiny moonbeam hair. I met his eyes instead. They weren't nearly as appealing. When he looked into mine, I could tell he knew something was wrong.

"What happened?" *Can you talk in front of the others? Do we need to go to my office?*

Not right now, I need more information first. "Nate happened."

I heard the groans from around the table. Cassie looked around confused. Eric wasn't paying attention, so I filled her in.

"Nate has a habit of abusing his fated mate."

She frowned and then looked at Eric. "Is he the one you told me about?" Her voice betrayed her worry and anxiety.

My non-observant brother put it towards the incident on hand. He rubbed his hand across the back of her neck. Her spine stiffened slightly. Eric looked confused and stopped.

My wolf growled in my head.

My father looked at me. As the Alpha, he had a connection to each of our wolves.

All this happened within the same three seconds it took before Eric answered her question.

"Yes, he is."

"Father, we need you and Eric to go see Allie in the hospital. Break their bond." My comment was met with four startled gasps. It was rare and only under extreme circumstances. I forced myself to look only at him and not her.

"She wasn't healing, she had bruises all over her body that were old. This time he had thrown her against a wall, knocking her out. The paramedics and I found a bottle of wolfsbane in their house. He must have been poisoning her to keep her from healing. He is not going to stop until he kills her one day. He is trying to make her as weak as him."

My father aged ten years in that moment. No one wanted to take away someone's right to a fated mate.

Well, not willingly anyway.

From the look of things across the table, my own brother was about to take mine. I couldn't think about that now though.

My father pushed himself up, regretfully. "Come on, Eric. Your wolf is strong enough we should be able to do this. Bea, will you come with us? Allie is going to need someone to support her."

Mom stood up too, only she was more forceful and determined than my father. Knowing her, she was probably thinking of going over to the station to teach Nate a lesson or two about tough love.

My eyes were on Eric and Cassie though. He bent down and kissed the top of her head, a slight crease in his eyebrows told me that was not what he was expecting. At least he had enough sense to know there was trouble in paradise.

My wolf continued to growl unhappily every time Eric touched her.

My father stopped when he was about to pass me and looked me in the eyes.

You and I are talking when I get back.

Yes, father.

He studied me a moment longer, then walked outside.

"Hey, little brother! Guess it's my turn to run off to work." Eric gave me an enthusiastic hug, which I struggled to return. "Do me a favor, keep an eye on Cassie for me." He winked at me, just like the cocky idiot that he was.

Truthfully, I loved my brother, and he was one of my best friends. We had our differences, but that was fine. It kept things interesting. I was just a little frustrated with the current circumstances.

I smiled at him. "No worries, big brother. I'll take better care of her than you ever could."

He cackled his whole way out the door, closing it behind him. The room felt like someone hit pause, until we heard the car start pulling away. Then time started moving again.

I turned as Cassie stood up from her chair.

"I...uh. I need to go call my mom. I forgot to tell her when we got here yesterday, she's probably going crazy."

Without thinking I reached out and grabbed her wrist as she passed. My wolf howled softly at the shock of electricity that ran between us. Her breath caught, she felt it too. I looked up from where I was holding her and noticed the small tear escaping from her eye.

Without a moment's hesitation. I pulled her in and held her tight to me. I heard her sniffle and then take a deep breath, inhaling my scent. Her body immediately settled, and she held me tighter back. We stood like that for so long, and yet for such a short amount of time. I never wanted to let her go.

She was mine, dang it!

"We can't do this." She began crying again.

I expected her to push me away again, she did the opposite, she held me tighter.

"Why can't we? You're my fated mate. You belong with me. You know that. You felt the bond start last night, and you feel it now."

"I do. I can't deny that. But I'm also Eric's chosen mate."

I shook my head. "Not yet, you're not. Not until he asks, not until you let him…" I had to practically rip the words out of my mouth to finish, "claim you." I grimaced as I said it.

My wolf growled. We didn't like the idea of anyone else claiming our mate. She looked up at me, her eyes overflowing in tears. I reached down and wiped one from under her eye.

"What do you want, Cassie? What Eric wants, what I want, that's not what's important here. What do you want?"

Something I said pushed her over the edge and she began sobbing.

"I don't know what I want. Before yesterday, I thought it was Eric. I thought I was okay with accepting a chosen mate. But then he…" She shook her head, stopping herself from finishing whatever she was going to say. "But then I met you, and last night was… it was…" She hiccupped and cried too hard to finish the rest.

"Perfect?" I smiled down and kissed her forehead.

Her body shivered as I pressed my lips to her skin. She nodded, unable to speak again.

"What did he do, Cas?"

She shook her head. The fact that she didn't want to tell me made me worry. I knew my brother and I knew everything he had told me about her.

"Did he get impatient with you? Did he try to push you?"

She creased her brows and looked at me quizzically. I smirked. It was absolutely adorable. I couldn't help it, not that I tried even the slightest, I had to kiss the little crease.

"He tells me everything, more than I want to know most of the time." I sighed. I really didn't want to tell her about all the times he's bragged to me about his *conquests*.

She gave a little huff, her breath washed over my neck, sending more goosebumps through my body. My wolf sighed at the undiluted batch of her scent.

"He didn't mean to. His wolf just took over."

My throat tightened, my words came out clipped and rough. "What did he do?"

On instinct, Cassie moved her arms around my neck and held me close to her. My nose was next to her neck, where I took in as much of her scent as I could, calming my wolf and I back down.

The reason why she had to comfort me was fighting the soothing sensation though, bringing the urge to strangle my brother back up again..

"Cassie?" I pushed her for more.

Her voice was soft and shaky. "He tried to use his Alpha command on me, trying to force me to mate. Since I'm not part of your pack, it didn't work the way he wanted it too. My wolf went on the offensive and came out. She told him off and made him feel guilty enough that Eric was able to fight for control again. He spent half the car ride here lecturing his wolf."

I couldn't respond to her because my wolf was fighting me for control this time. He wanted to go rip into our older brother, our future Alpha.

I felt her moving but was too focused on holding him back that I wasn't paying attention. Not until two gentle palms were on my cheeks and she was turning my face toward hers.

"I'm okay. He didn't hurt me. Nothing happened. In fact, I told him he needed to lay off for a while, take a step back. Give his wolf time to chill out." She kissed my cheek and my wolf immediately melted into a big puddle of mental fur. "I'm okay, Ricky."

I loved the sound of my name on her lips. I loved the feel of my lips on hers even more. She gave a small gasp when I went in for it. Which was the only negative response she had.

I thought she would push me away, or that I would have to coax her, but no. She needed this as much as I did.

We pulled away a few heavenly spent minutes later, completely breathless, but left our foreheads together. "Tell me what you want, Cassie. You are my mate. I will give you whatever you need."

She gave a small hum, and her eyes were closed. Her contentment didn't last though. "I don't know. No matter what I choose, no matter what happens, I am going to hurt someone."

I shook my head. "Bonds die when you are claimed."

"Bonds may die but feelings don't. If I choose him, you will feel the rejection. You will always remember that I chose him. You will always remember how good this felt together. Even if you were to claim another, it would always be there. If I chose you, there is no bond to erase with him. We created that. It will not go away. His feelings will still be there. Bitterness is going to fester on either end. What will happen between you two? Your brotherhood? Your friendship?" Her voice cracked in the end.

I held her head against my chest, finally hearing what she was saying. It wasn't as simple as her making a choice and us moving on. Nothing was ever simple where Eric was concerned, not unless you agreed to his way.

"I need time, Ricky. I need space to figure this out. Maybe I should leave."

"No!" It was a knee jerk reaction. It also came out in a growl, as it was from both my wolf and me. I softened my voice. "Sorry, neither my wolf nor I want you to leave. We'd rather give you your space, with you still here. As I said. Whatever you need, my love. You are our mate. We are here to provide for you."

A small sob broke through again. I wanted to say more, hold her longer, but our time was up. We both jumped when we heard the sounds of a car coming down the road. Her eyes lit up in panic and it killed me.

"Go to your room. I'll tell them you are taking a nap, that you are still tired. That should buy you some time."

She gave me a soft smile, then quickly jumped up and kissed me. "Thank you."

And with that she flew up the stairs.

I stayed in the kitchen and pulled myself together. I wiped my eyes as I walked to the fridge, acting like I was looking for something to eat, when food was the last thing on my mind.

"Well, that was an interesting experience. I really hope to never have to do that again." Eric's loud voice came from the entryway and down the hall.

I grabbed the jug of orange juice from the fridge and set it on the counter as he came in. He looked around the room and frowned.

"Where's Cassie?" He did sound a little concerned about her at least, I had to give him that.

I mentally gave myself a shake. I listened to him talk about this female for months. I knew how much he cared about her. Which just made all of this harder. It would have been easier had he been a complete tool and just been using her.

"She, uh. Said she was still tired, so she went to lay down."

The crease above his eyes deepened as he headed for the hall.

"Eric?" I called him back. He stopped and looked at me, annoyed that I had the nerve to stop him. "Let her be, man. She'll come down when she is ready."

I saw the torn look on his face as he internally debated, and then caved. He was growing, good for him.

He probably remembered how out of control his wolf is when it comes to her and decided she was safer with him down here. My wolf grumbled.

More than likely. But at least he is thinking about someone else's feelings for a change.

All I got back was a disgruntled harumph.

I poured myself a glass of juice, put the jug back in the fridge, and then took a seat across from my older brother and best friend. The silence was agonizing.

"So? What'd you think of Cas?" His grin grew, making him look like a dog begging for a treat. The mental image made me smirk.

"I like her, she's really great, just like you said."

You have no idea how much we like her.

Will you shut up? Not helping me here. We can't let on about any of it until she is ready. Whatever Cassie needs, remember?

Eric sighed and scratched his jawline, a smile playing on his face. He opened his mouth to say more, probably something that was going to make this day even more difficult, but he was cut off by our father walking in the room.

"Ricky? Let's go have that chat now. I need to hear all the details about last night."

I nodded and stood up, finishing off my juice as I carried it to the sink. I stopped and pointed at Eric before leaving.

"I know you, Eric. Leave her alone. After yesterday you owe her some space."

Smooth.

Shut up, it slipped.

Eric's jaw dropped. He glanced at our father's retreating back in the hall.

"She told you about that?"

I shrugged like it wasn't a big deal, an idea came to me, and I decided to run with it. "I must have one of those faces that makes people feel the need to confide in me. You always give me *way* too much information."

He snorted and nodded with a proud grin.

Such a cocky jerk. Why do we love him again?

Because blood has forced us too.

Right.

"She needs space, Eric. Go for a run, let your wolf burn off some of his stress."

Eric nodded eagerly, like I was giving him the best news in the world. He stood up and patted my shoulder.

"Thanks, little brother. You are wise beyond your years."

I rolled my eyes behind his back and watched him leave out the back patio door.

I took a deep breath then joined my father in his office. He was already behind his desk waiting for me. I closed the door behind me, mentally preparing myself for what I knew I was going to have to tell him.

"Sit." He commanded, pointing at the chair across from him. As soon as I sat down, he gave another command. "Spill."

I could have played dumb. I could have acted like I didn't know what he was talking about. I could have told him every detail of what went down with Nate. But no. I knew what he wanted. And truth be told. I needed to talk to someone who wasn't involved in it.

I spent the next twenty minutes pouring my heart out to my Alpha father. I told him all about last night and all about this morning. The only time he said anything was when I got to this morning, and when I realized who my mate was.

I didn't hear my father curse often, so I was more than a little surprised when it came out of his mouth.

"What do I do dad? How do I fix this?"

He shook his head sadly. "You can't, plain and simple. Keep doing what you're doing. Let her have the space and time. Wish I could tell Eric to do the same. But she's right. The volcano is going to explode when everything comes out. No one can make this choice for her. And no one can pressure her into it. And we both know your brother is great with putting pressure on things. I'm not even sure if I can give you advice because then I would be taking sides."

He gave a deep sigh and leaned back in his chair. After a few moments of quiet thinking, he continued.

"I'm not picking sides between my sons." I nodded, not surprised by that. "But I will always pick the side of fate. I wasn't much different than Eric when I was younger. I have no doubts that I was too stupid to pick what was best for me. If it hadn't been for fate intervening, I probably would have let her get away. Now, you and Cassie. Neither of you are that stupid. You would have found each other eventually. I like the female. She has a good strong head on those shoulders. I'm not siding with either son, I am siding with fate. Fate is a weird thing. Take Nathan for instance. He was given a precious gift, but he didn't appreciate it. He didn't respect what he was given. He tried to force it into something it wasn't. He screwed with his own fate. Keep that in mind. Don't try to pressure or force fate into your will. Let it come on its own."

"So, sit back and let Cassie drive the boat?" I think I understood what he was saying, but… I was lost.

He pointed at me emphatically. "Exactly!"

Ya huh. Alright. I stood up. "Thanks, dad. I think."

He chuckled as I walked back out the door.

I entered the family room at the same time Cassie was coming down the stairs.

CHAPTER 14

Cassie

I ran my butt up those stairs like the hounds of hell were chasing me. I was grateful for Ricky's suggestion. Too much happened in the last few days. It was all just too much.

I laid down on my bed and pulled the pillow up and over, smothering myself. I hardly slept at all last night. Meeting Ricky had been exactly like the dream I had months ago, before my first date with Eric.

The chasing, the playing, the kissing. The male.

I had shifted back because I realized what we were doing, I realized who he was to me. I was so freaked out I didn't know what else to do. Then I saw his face. I knew that face. That moment was when I remembered the dream.

I should have stayed and talked to him last night. I shouldn't have run.

No, you should have stayed and let him claim us last night.

That wouldn't have helped anything, and you know it. It probably would have made things worse.

Pfft.

Eric may not be perfect, but he has been good to us. He does love us. You can't deny that.

I won't accept anyone but our fated mate.

Yeah, I knew she was going to say that. And I couldn't blame her.

You heard everything Ricky said downstairs, Cas. He wants what we want. He is putting aside his feelings to provide for us. Would Eric do the same? If you had told him what happened, how would he have responded?

I grumbled, not wanting to answer her. Not that my silence was going to stop her.

Exactly, you know it as well as I do. He would have pushed for us to mate before the bond set in. Eric thinks of himself first, and then others. That's a lesson he is going to have to learn. Her tone softened as I began sniffling again. *We have to let him go, Cas.*

I know that. I also know that I do still love him enough that I don't want to hurt him. What I told Ricky is still true. You know we are going to be the bomb that destroys this family. This pack.

She had nothing to add to that, she knew I was right. On some level, she still loved Eric too. It was odd though. I felt like I loved him less today than I did this time yesterday.

Was that the fate bond?

Was it already wiping away my feelings for Eric?

Would that happen for Eric if I let Ricky claim me?

Or would it go away for Ricky if I let Eric have the claim?

Doesn't matter. It takes both of us in a mating. I refuse to participate for anyone but Ricky, our true mate.

I couldn't blame her. From everything Eric told me about Ricky, he was probably our better match. At least we wouldn't have to keep reminding him to think of other people and not just himself.

Eric did have a big heart, he cared about other people, he just forgot sometimes... I think. I'd seen how much he cared about his brother and Jordan. And me. But even then, he would still put himself before everyone else.

I jumped when I heard the back door open and close. I looked out the window and saw Eric strip down right there, not caring if anyone else was watching, then he shifted and took off for the woods.

How much do you wanna bet that was Ricky's doing? He convinced Eric to leave us be and to go for a run.

I sighed and sat back down. *You're probably right.*

She scoffed. *Duh, I always am.*

I couldn't help the small laugh passing through my lips. I leaned over and picked up my phone. I needed to talk to Yolanda.

"Miss me already? It's only been like...36 hours."

I laughed and then I started crying. Only that long?

"Uh oh, what happened?"

I sniffled and wiped my nose with the back of my hand as I walked to the bathroom in search of a tissue.

"You can't tell anything I am about to tell you to Jordan. Swear to me, Yo. He can't know any of this yet."

"I would never break your trust like that, and he doesn't have access to my head yet, so we're in the clear. Just hold on a sec." I listened as she excused herself from the room and moved to another one. She didn't speak again until the door closed behind her. "Okay, we're in the clear. Spill!"

"I...uh." I cleared my throat and pulled my nerves together. "I met my fated mate." Yolanda sucked air in through her teeth, making a backward hissing noise. "Oh, just wait, it gets even better. Are you sitting down?"

"No... should I be?" She asked carefully and suspiciously.

"Yeah." My voice cracked again. I waited for her to tell me she was sitting, then continued. "It's Eric's younger brother, his best friend, his future Gamma. Ricky."

The line was silent for so long, I looked at my phone to make sure my call hadn't dropped.

"Are you still there?"

"Ya huh, just trying to decide if this is some horrible prank or not, because if it is, then we need to work on your funny bone because this is far from funny."

I started crying again, which seemed to help her believe it. A few colorful curse words flew out of her mouth, followed by a knock on a door from her end. I could hear Jordan's muffled voice and then Yolanda assuring him that everything was fine. He didn't believe her but went away anyway.

"Alright, he's gone. I need to hear everything if I am going to help you with this."

I told her everything, from the scent in the hall, to letting him chase me. I even told her about what happened with Eric's wolf, she muttered the curse words this time.

"The weirdest thing is, I can already feel my feelings for Eric fading."

"Yeah, hon. That's all part of the bond. I never told you about this male I dated years ago. I was devastated when he met his fated mate. It was why I chose to go to school in Seattle, I needed a break from him. I harbored those feelings all these years, up until I met Jordan, then they were just… gone."

"I was right then. Eric's feelings are not just going to disappear because Ricky marks me. Instead, it's going to make everything worse." I gasped, realizing I just officially picked one of the brothers.

"And from that sound I am assuming you had been sitting on the edge of the fence, refusing to pick a side, and now you've fallen over without meaning to."

"Ya huh. What do I do, Yo?"

I listened to her breathe, picturing the way she paces when she was thinking hard about something, her fingers drumming on her leg. Then I heard the huff of disappointment. I knew what she was going to say.

"I have no idea what to tell you."

"Part of me wants to just leave, like right now."

"I get that, but don't. Not yet at least. Keep doing what you're doing for now. Keep distance from both of them. Eric is going to make that hard. Ricky will try to honor that distance, but your wolf is going to push you to go to him. I do not envy you at all, right now."

I looked out the window when I saw movement from the corner of my eye. Eric was sauntering back, still in wolf form. Which meant his eyesight was even better and he saw me. He sped up to get to the patio and shifted back faster.

"I gotta go. Eric is back from his run and spotted me through the window. No more faking sleep."

"Alright, good luck, keep me updated."

"Thanks, Yo."

I hung up, slid my phone in my pocket and wiped my eyes. I did a quick check in the mirror, just to make sure I still looked like crap. Which I did. At least I was succeeding at one thing.

Walking down those stairs felt like walking down the hall to death row.

My heart stuttered when I smelled Ricky, just seconds before I saw him. He was coming down the hall on the first floor, the one that led to the Alpha and Beta's offices. My eyes met his and he smiled. My breathing slowed, and everything felt like it was sliding into place.

Then Eric walked into the living room, arms wide open, running right at me. From the corner of my eye, I saw Ricky tense. His fists opening and closing. His wolf didn't like that. Neither did mine for that matter.

Eric lifted me up and spun me around as soon as he got to me.

I knew he was going to try and kiss me again, and just like this morning, I looked down, forcing him to kiss the top of my head. I felt more than I saw his pout.

At one time, I thought it was cute when he pouted. Now? It was really annoying.

Would it have always reached this point eventually? Or was it only because Ricky showed up and fate forced my hands?

Didn't matter. There was no going back.

Maybe I only fell in love with Eric because he was the first real boyfriend I had ever had. He made me feel alive, loved, and wanted. I knew he loved me, but I didn't think it would have been enough to get me through the rest of our lives.

Before he could ask what was wrong... again, my phone buzzed. I pulled it out and stepped away from him when I saw Yolanda's name.

Yo: Just remembered. Girl, you need to get out of there before Christmas. Trust me, it will be better for everyone if you are. He had *special* plans if you know what I mean.

I turned the screen off on my phone and closed my eyes. If this had been last week, if he had asked me before we left, I would have said yes in a heartbeat. Christmas was in four days. This either had to be over by then, or I had to leave by then.

I felt Eric's hand hit my lower back. I tried not to do it, I did, but I failed. My back stiffened. I tried to pass it off as though he startled me.

"Everything alright, sweetheart?" He sounded so worried, it pulled at my heartstrings, the few left that still belonged to him.

That little bit of me wanted to reassure him by laying my head on his chest.

Unfortunately, I was also very aware of Ricky standing there. All 6 foot 4 inches of him. His teal eyes watched me carefully, or rather, his brother's hand on my back.

The scowl didn't fit his face. He had the face of someone who thought through each of their decisions. They did not act rashly, only smartly. Until then, he would school his face, and no one else would know how he felt.

Which was exactly what he did before Eric turned around. His face went blank, not letting his brother see how badly he was hurting him. I could see it though. I could see the pain in his eyes, and then I saw that switch to worry for me. Because he was reacting to the pain he saw in mine.

This was ridiculous. I just wanted to throw my hands in the air and walk away.

"Cas?"

"Huh?" I turned to look at Eric again. Right, he had asked me a question. I shook my head. "Yeah, sorry. Just a message from Yolanda checking in. You know how she worries about me."

Eric chuckled and wrapped his arm around my waist. "Yeah, she treats you like a little sister, even though you are nearly the same age."

Just the mention of sisters, mixed with my already vulnerable emotions, had me closing my eyes. I bet Katie would have been great at navigating the awkward situation I found myself in. She would have known what to do.

When I opened my eyes again, Ricky gave me that investigator look. He was watching me carefully. He caught my reaction. He knew there was a story there. My eyes watered. Not now!

I forced myself to listen to whatever Eric was saying.

"I bet you would have loved to have a sister, huh? Another female around the house."

I pushed him away, a little offended at his words, even though I didn't know why. "I already have a sister, thank you."

Eric rolled his eyes. "I meant a blood sister, Cas. Yolanda doesn't actually count."

I looked at him, confused at what he was saying. Did I really never tell him about Katie? We'd been together for nearly five months, and I never told him about my brother's twin sister? The sister who died saving my life?

How was that possible? I shook my head and stepped away, heading for the back door.

"Cas? What did I say? Come on. Talk to me."

Gah! Had he always whined this much?

Eric followed me out, and I was pretty sure Ricky was following right behind him. There was no way he was going to leave me when he could see my distress.

I didn't stop at the patio. I just kept walking. Maybe I would go for a run.

I felt Eric grab my arm and turn me around. "Cas?" It was a demand, yet a plea at the same time.

I forced a half smile. "I'm fine. I'm just tired and need some air."

I patted his hand wrapped around my arm. He loosened it enough that I was able to pull away. I started walking into the field again. My pace wasn't too fast, I could still hear the brothers arguing behind me.

"Let her be, Eric. You heard her. She just needs air and space."

"But… I can't… Not alone. She doesn't know these woods."

My wolf scoffed. *If only he knew how well we knew these woods.*

I could sense her irritation. She was just as upset about the sister comment as I was. She never got to meet our sister, but she had seen my memories of her. She was a little disgruntled about that.

"I'll talk to her, okay."

Eric growled not so softly. "Fine. Eventually she is going to have to talk to me though."

"Not with that attitude she won't."

I didn't hear Eric's response, having sped up to get out of ear shot. I did hear Ricky running to catch up to me though.

I was just about to the trees when I felt his presence. I stopped walking and looked back up at him. I could see Eric pacing on the patio, about the middle of each pass he would look up at us.

"Do you want to talk here or keep going? He can't hear us from this distance, but he can see us."

I pressed my lips together. "If we disappear, he will come looking for us."

Ricky nodded. "True. So, you wanna tell me what that was all about. I could tell something about that sister thing bothered you, I just don't know why. If you want to talk about it, I'm right here."

My eyes gravitated to his. I smiled softly and opened my mouth to speak. Before I could though, Ricky was moving around me and shoving me behind him.

"What are you doing here, Nate? Who let you out of jail?" I had never heard such venom come from Ricky's mouth before. Or anybody's really.

"Thought you said you didn't have a mate, Rick?" The clearly crazy male tried taunting him. Nate was shorter than Ricky and weighed less than half of him. The male was obviously stupid as well as crazy.

"I didn't at the time. Now, who let you out?"

Nate shrugged. "I made bail. My pops may not have been good for much, but he was at least good enough for that."

I heard footsteps running up behind us, but I was too afraid to look away from what was going on in front of me.

It was an odd sensation. I was standing right there in the backyard, a full-grown adult, watching Ricky protect me. But I was also standing in a large, wooded area, five years old, watching my eight-year-old siblings fight off a skinny wolf with foam coming out of his mouth.

My grip on Ricky's shirt tightened, fear for his life, the way I watched it leave my sister, ran through me.

"What's going on?" Eric commanded.

Even if I knew, I wouldn't have been able to respond. The crazy man lifted a gun toward the fated mate I just found.

At the same time, Ricky pushed me into Eric and shifted. Eric twisted us to the ground on some signal I hadn't heard. Ricky shifted midair as the gun went off.

"Ricky!" I screamed, completely freaked.

There was no way this was happening again. I struggled to push Eric off me, but the large giant of a male would not budge.

"I need to get to him!"

"No, you need to stay right here. Ricky's fine."

"No, no one else is dying to protect me. Not this time."

Well, that seemed to have gotten Eric's attention. He looked down at me, totally confused and lost.

"Cas…"

I lifted a finger. "No, I do not want to talk about it and now is not the time." From the corner of my eye, I saw Ricky shift back and collapse onto the ground. "Let me go, so I can help your brother. He's hurt and I am the most qualified person here."

I heard more voices coming from the house. Eric looked up at who was coming and then back to his brother. I saw a trace of fear cross his eyes as he rolled off me.

I did a mix of crawling and running to get to Ricky. I placed my hands on his cheeks, and he looked up at me.

"I'm alright. I promise. I'm not ready to leave you yet."

I snorted. Well, at least they both had lame jokes in common.

I carefully examined his body, looking for where the bullet got him. I sighed with extreme relief when I saw he had only been grazed, a deep graze, but a graze, nonetheless. It was deep enough that he was bleeding, but not deep enough to need stitches. Maybe if he was human he would have, but not for a shifter.

"The bullet just grazed you. We'll get you back into the house and I can clean it up. It should be healed within the hour." He nodded and laid his head back on the grass.

I reached and grabbed a piece of his torn clothing off the ground and pressed it against his side to stop the bleeding. He hissed and flinched, but otherwise didn't say a word. I looked around and saw Charles and Eric next to Nate.

Bea came and knelt on Ricky's other side. Her hands moved across his face, the same way mine had.

"How is he?" She asked me.

I smiled. "It's just a graze. He'll be fine. If the other two can help move him into his room, I can clean out the wound and bandage it."

"Are you sure he shouldn't go to the hospital?"

I tried to tell myself Eric wasn't doubting my abilities, he was just worried about his brother. It didn't help.

I scowled at him, and he flinched. "I was raised in a family of pack doctors. If I wasn't at school, then I was in the hospital helping my parents. My mother is a nurse, my father is a pack doctor. My grandfather before him, his grandfather before him. My brother is in his residency. I don't actually need the medical classes. Those are just to make the human government happy. Now, shut up, lift up your brother, and carry him to his room, or I will give *you* a reason to go to the hospital."

Both Bea and Eric's jaws hit the grass. Charles on the other hand was grinning ear to ear as he gave the order. "You heard the female. Let's get this male inside."

Eric was still shocked and dumbfounded as he helped his father lift up Ricky and carry him.

I felt Bea's arm go around my waist, almost like she was lending me her strength. "Bravo, Cassie. Bravo."

She kissed the side of my head and walked through the door before me.

Bea moved to the kitchen, and I went up the stairs. I had a pretty good idea of which room was Ricky's, odds were it was the one I always smelled him the strongest at.

I froze in his doorway. Eric and Charles were arguing.

"Dad, surely we should at least have Dr. Shapiro come over and check this out?"

Charles put a steadying hand on Eric's shoulder. "Son, I know you are worried about your brother. I've been around long enough myself to tell you that Cassie is right. It's just a graze. All it needs is cleaning and bandaging. I trust her hands better than ours." Charles patted Eric on the shoulder, turning him back around.

I squared my shoulders right before Eric saw me. "Cas, I didn't mean that I didn't have faith in you. I just…"

I let him off the hook and nodded. "Go clean up outside. I'll take care of Ricky." I looked at Charles, ignoring Eric altogether. "Would you have Bea bring up pure alcohol and something for bandages?"

Eric huffed and walked out. Charles chuckled. "She's already on it." He looked down the hall, making sure Eric was gone. "Besides medical training, you are still the best person for this. Our mates always are."

I tilted my head. "How?" I looked to where Ricky lay. He wasn't as asleep as he had been pretending. I saw the small smirk. "He told you."

"Eh, I didn't give him much of a choice. I'm honestly surprised no one else caught on with all the tension in the kitchen this morning." This time it was the Alpha who was kissing my head. "Take care of my pup, doc." I smirked as he walked out, closing the door behind him.

As soon as the door was closed, Ricky raised the arm on his right side, the one without the gunshot wound. I immediately stepped forward, going right to him. My hand slid inside his, looking like it was being swallowed up by a giant five-legged spider.

With my other hand, I lifted the falling bloody cloth again and pressed it against him.

"How are you?"

I laughed, unbelievable. He was the one that got shot, yet he was worried about me? I shook my head. "I'm fine, you're the one with a hole in his side."

He tskd. "This is nothing." I heard him take a shaky breath and watched him hold it in for a count of four before pushing it out. "Hearing you scream, not knowing if the bullet hit you too, it…" he cursed, which sounded kind of hot with his gravelly voice right now. "It scared me, Cas."

I had no free hand to wipe away his tears, so I settled for kissing the back of the hand I was holding.

"I'm fine. Really. I was just worried about you. I heard the shot, and then I saw you fall." I wanted to smack my head. "I didn't even ask what happened to the other guy."

Ricky chuckled softly and then groaned. "Pretty sure my wolf broke his neck. I had just enough time to mind-link Eric and tell him to catch you and drop you to the ground. I'm glad he had enough sense to cover you as well. My wolf saw the gun and flipped. Neither of us liked the idea of you and a loaded gun so close together."

I grasped his hand as tight as I could. "Well, I guess you proved you could protect us. My wolf is very impressed with you right now."

You got that right. I told you he was the one for us.

Ricky smiled, then raised my hand to kiss it.

I jumped when I heard the door open. He regretfully let go of my hand. Thankfully it was just his mother, with a tray loaded down with things.

"Alright, we have alcohol, bandages, cleaning cloths, water, a basin to soak said cleaning cloths in the said water. I also have a sandwich for you young lady, and soup for the holey man on the bed."

Ricky and I both laughed. I followed her to the other side of the bed, where she was setting the tray down. I saw her hands shaking and realized humor was her way of trying to hide her fears. I gripped both her hands in mine and waited until she looked up to meet my eyes.

I didn't say anything, I knew she didn't want Ricky to know how worried she was. I just gave her what I hoped was a reassuring smile.

"Thank you, Bea. This is perfect. And I'm starving, so thank you for the food too."

A tear fell down her cheek, which she brushed away quickly and cleared her throat. "Alright, well, I will leave you to it. We'll try to keep Eric out of your hair. Big brothers are horrible when their younger siblings get hurt."

"Ha! Tell me about it." I didn't think she noticed the shake in my voice. It was funny at first. Pat was always worried when I got hurt. But then I remembered Katie. And it wasn't so funny anymore.

Bea gave a small wave as she closed the door behind her. I imagined she was also taking a minute in the hall to pull herself together.

I poured the water in the basin and soaked a cloth. I twisted it, making sure all the excess water was out of it, then carried it over to the left side of his bed. I purposely ignored the intense gaze I felt following my every move.

I carefully pulled the dirty and bloody makeshift bandage I had been using, off his skin. That broke Ricky's concentration on me. He hissed and closed his eyes, turning his face away from me.

I frowned. It had been nearly twenty minutes since he got hit. There should have been at least a small amount of healing. Why wasn't there?

"What's wrong? And don't say nothing. I can see it in your eyes. What's wrong?"

"Your wound. It should have started healing by now. But it's not." I gently laid the wet cloth against it and started wiping away the blood. "It still looks fresh, as though it just happened. I don't understand. Maybe Eric was right, maybe we should have Dr. Shapiro come help."

"No. He's not. You were right. You're the only person I want helping me."

I sighed and stood up, moving to rinse the cloth off and get a real bandage for him. "You're biased. I don't know why you aren't healing, Ricky."

"I do." He snorted. "Nate most likely dipped the bullet in wolfsbane. We know he used it on his mate. I probably missed a bottle somewhere. We didn't keep looking after we found the one in the cabinet. It was a rookie mistake."

Right, I knew that. I should have thought of that. Think Cassie.

"There is no real way to rid your body of the wolfsbane. You're just going to have to let it pass through. Since it was just a graze, it didn't go far into your system. In fact, you will probably just bleed it out. Blood works as a natural cleanser. It pushes the dirt and germs out, cleaning the wound. This is going to take longer than an hour though. Possibly several. Depending on how much poison got into your system."

By that point I was already placing the first of what would be many bandages, on his side. I taped it and went to wash my hands in the basin.

CHAPTER 15

Ricky

I watched as the exotic looking being cleaned my side, trying not to hurt me, and bandaged my wound. If I learned anything over the last few days, it was that fate definitely knew what she was doing.

My father was right as well. Even without fate's help, I would have chosen Cassie.

I could see what drew my brother to her. She was strong. She was smart. She was gentle. She was more stubborn than him. And she was selfless.

Of course, we couldn't forget the most obvious of everything she was, an absolute goddess.

I didn't need all this attention for my wound. It wasn't the first graze I'd had. It wasn't even the first time I'd been shot. I knew how to take care of it myself, my parents did as well. But there was no way I was passing up the opportunity to have my mate to myself, without the need to sneak around.

I did need her for other reasons though.

My wolf was still anxious about her being in danger. We had been able to feel her incredible fear of what was happening. We felt it to our core. We needed to have her nearby, it was the only way I would be able to keep him calm.

Keeping her out of Eric's reach is helpful too. When can we tell him, so he stops touching our mate?

I don't know. That's up to Cassie. You heard our father, our Alpha. We can't push her.

She wants to be with us. Her wolf is calling to us. She is here for us. She doesn't even like him touching her.

I know. It's more complicated than it should be. For the sake of the pack, this needs to be handled carefully.

He gave me a low grunt. I sighed and rubbed my head, trying to will my body to relax. I felt a light touch pressing down on the bandages and turned my head. Cassie had returned to the chair next to me.

How could this beautiful female be mine?

"Tell me about your sister." I reached out and took her hand in mine again.

Her head shot up. "Who said I had a sister?" Her lip barely curled up on the edge, the challenge clear in her eyes.

My wolf growled appreciatively. She wasn't going to make anything easy on us.

I raised an eyebrow. "Really?"

That same little lip started quivering just a bit. My hand, with hers still encased in it, lifted of its own accord, and traced that bottom lip. Her eyes closed and I felt the deep breath slide out of her lips and across my fingers.

"Tell me… please?" My voice was soft, trying to keep the command out of it.

She cleared her throat, which was my cue to lower our hands.

"I have an older brother, Patrick Jr. When we were kids, he had a twin sister." There had been a ghost of a smile, a shaky one, but enough so that I knew there had been good memories before whatever happened.

"Her name was Katie." Cassie sniffled and gave a small laugh. "I looked up to Katie. I followed her around everywhere she went. She was only three years older than me, but to me, she was the bravest and the smartest. Katie never cared if I followed her around, just like the pup I was. She had the sweetest soul. Over the years, my memories have dimmed of her. But I will never forget the way she made me feel. How she always made me feel like I was important. What I remember most," and here her smile grew higher, "was her letting me lay out in the yard with her, watching the stars." She gave another small laugh.

"Katie was always watching the stars. She said they brought her peace and tranquility. I realize how odd that probably sounded coming from a small pup, but that was Katie in a nutshell. She had one of those old souls."

I let Cassie have a moment, as she tried to pull herself together.

"What happened to her?" I mean, come on. It was obvious Katie wasn't around anymore.

The tears were running hard now. "When I was five, a large group of rogues attacked our pack. I had been out playing in the trees. Our parents ran out to help the injured. It didn't take long for our pack to take them down. The rogues knew what they were doing though, they spread out, trying to cover more territory. I didn't hear one of them until it was too late. He was right there in front of me. I was scared stiff, I couldn't move. I'll never forget the dirty, disheveled look he had. The male was wearing some type of loincloth. It was like watching a movie in slow motion as he shifted into his wolf. His cloth just fell as he shifted, lying there, waiting for him to pick it up again. I couldn't even scream as I watched him run at me. His wolf was skinny, a sickly-looking kind of skinny. He had this foam looking stuff coming out of his jaws."

A not so small shiver went through her. All I wanted was to reach out and hold her in my arms, it wasn't what she needed from me at that moment though. I tightened my grip on her hand, and she released another shaky breath.

"Before the rogue made it to me, a fiery ball with long black hair came shooting out of the trees nearby. She hit him straight in the side with her shoulder, knocking him off balance. Katie was only eight, but her strength had been increasing. My mom used to tease her that she was going to hit puberty and get her wolf soon. Right behind Katie came Pat. When they'd heard about the rogues, they came to search for me. They couldn't do much, but they were able to hold off the wolf until help could come. My feet were still rooted to the same spot, no matter how many times Katie yelled at me to run. Her last time was cut off. The rogue hit her hard with his head, flinging her into a tree. A moment later, a pack warrior arrived and finished him off. Unfortunately, it was too late for Katie. She never woke up."

I raised her hand up to my lips and softly kissed it. I was just about to pull her out of her chair and into my arms, but my wolf stopped me.

Don't. That will make her feel weak. She needs to feel strong. Just keep talking to her. That's what they need.

"Did you go back to being five today? When I had you behind me?"

"Partially. It was like I was in both places at the same time." She gave a small hiccup. "I thought I was going to lose you too. Females in our pack are trained along with the males. I know how to fight. I never wanted to be put in that position again." She snorted. "Not that that ever mattered to Pat. He was always overprotective, losing Katie just made it worse." She sighed, losing the all too short moment of levity. "In the end, it really didn't matter. I still froze behind you. I should have been able to get Eric away from me to get to you."

"Hey, no one expected you to solve the problem. Nate was my problem. His vendetta was against me. I hadn't taken him seriously enough when he threatened you yesterday."

"How could he threaten me? He didn't even know me."

I rubbed my lips together, debating how much to tell her.

Everything, we tell her everything.

"As far as Nate is, *was*, concerned, I am the reason he lost his mate. He threatened to make me pay. If he couldn't have his mate, then I couldn't have mine. I just laughed at him and told him good luck with that." I still couldn't believe I taunted him like that. I felt so much self-recrimination. "I hadn't met you yet. I took what he said with a grain of salt. That was just hours before I smelled you in this house."

I gave her a mock groan, like it had been such a hardship to smell her. "Do you know, I had to leave my own home because your smell was so strong, and we had no idea where it came from? My wolf was going insane."

She gave a lighthearted giggle. "I had the same problem. I kept catching faint whiffs of something chocolatey. It was worse when I passed your door on my way to bed. It was too weak for us to pinpoint what it was, but it was enough, mixed with the other events from that day, my wolf was practically bouncing in my head."

She laughed out loud, and I gave her a curious look. She shook her head softly, her loose hair waving around her chin, like a curtain blowing in the breeze.

Cassie tapped the side of her head. "She's grumbling over the term *bouncing.*"

I opened my mouth to say something else, possibly to tease her wolf some more. I was cut off when we heard the door open. She dropped my hand and reached for the tape on my side.

In her haste to cover up the movement, she pulled on the tape a little too hard. I hissed, and not just from the pull of the small hairs.

It was from the interruption of my brother.

"Hey, how are you feeling, Rick?"

Eric walked up behind Cassie, placing his hand on her upper back, and bent over to look as she pulled a corner of the bandage down. He grimaced and I had to laugh.

Irritated, Eric. I felt very irritated. I had *almost* forgotten that he was the boulder blocking the path between my mate and I. *Almost.*

"Why does it still look so bad? I thought you said it would be healed in an hour?" Eric's accusatory voice grated against my nerves.

"Knock it off, Eric." I told him. "It's not her fault the moron dipped the bullet in wolfsbane first."

Eric stepped back, thankfully removing his hand from her so fast it was like I had hit him with a hot iron.

"What? See! You do need a hospital."

"No, he doesn't."

"Cas! He's still bleeding. He's not healing. This is going above what you know how to do."

I watched as Cassie slowly stood up and turned to him, an angry scowl on his face.

"Believe it or not, it's not always a bad thing when we bleed. That blood happens to be how the poison is exiting his system. I know what I am doing. Stop doubting my abilities." She shook her head as she passed him to grab the dirty cloth.

"I'll be back in a few minutes." She pointed at me sternly. It was terrifying and hot at the same time. "Don't move."

"Yes, ma'am."

She may not have smiled, but her lip did twitch.

We both watched as she left the room, closing the door behind her. Eric sank into her now vacated chair. He let out a shaky breath and rubbed both hands over his face.

"You scared the hell out of me, man."

"Thank you for responding so quickly. My wolf hadn't given me much notice before shifting."

"How did you know Nate was going to do something like that? All I saw from the porch was you pulling Cas behind you. I couldn't even see who you were talking to until I got there. Why did he come after you?"

Yeah... I wasn't telling him everything. "He wanted revenge. Nate blamed me for taking his mate away."

Eric nodded. "I get that." He turned and looked at the door, like Cassie was still there. "I'd probably lose it too, if someone tried to take my mate from me." He turned back to look at me with that sly, annoying smile. "I completely disagree with how he treated Allie, but a mate is a mate. It was rough breaking that bond." I watched as a painful look crossed my brother's face. He lifted his right arm and rubbed his chest. "I never expected for it to hurt us as well."

Neither did I.

"It left me with this extreme need to be near Cassie and reassure my wolf and I that she was here." Eric let out a sad sigh. "Not that it has mattered much. I thought she was over what happened the other day. She has been so distant though." His eyes bored into mine, pleading with me for help. "Has she said anything to you? I want to ask her about all these comments she's made today. Sister, someone dying to protect her. None of it makes any sense."

My heart did go out to my brother. The female he loved was pulling away from him. It was also becoming obvious that he really didn't know her all that well. He only knew the surface level of Cassie.

How did he not know her deeper levels after all this time?

I loved my brother, and I hated that I was part of what was hurting him. I was used to being able to talk things out with him. I didn't keep things from him.

Of course, he rarely flat out asked about me either. Not that he was asking about me now. He was asking about someone who was important to both of us.

I had to wonder though. Was he asking because he was worried about her and wanted to know everything about her?

Was he wanting to find a way to help her?

Or was it his pride that was hurt because he knew she hadn't told him something important to her?

Apparently I was silent too long, contemplating my own issues in this situation.

"She did, didn't she? Why was she able to confide in you and not me?"

My wolf scoffed. *Because she is our mate not yours.*

"It's simple. I asked. I asked without any ulterior motive. It had nothing to do with me or you, it only had to do with her. I know you care about her, but how often did you worry about her and what she wanted? And not what you wanted?"

Yeah, from the look on his face, he had no idea what I was talking about. I sighed, such a shame.

I grinned as the light of my life came back through the door. Cassie came in bearing a handful of towels. Without a word, she carried the bowl to my bathroom and dumped the bloody water out. Eric and I were both silent as she refilled the basin with the sink water.

"What, no more pure water?" I acted offended.

She tskd with her tongue. "Somebody certainly thinks highly of himself." She shook her head, dipping a new cloth in the water. "Water is water. Suck it up and deal with it."

Eric and I both chuckled. He moved out of the chair as she came back around. His hand rubbed her arm gently.

"Thank you for taking care of my brother, Cassie."

She smiled softly, if not awkwardly. "Of course." She turned her back to him and sat back down.

I was paying more attention to their interactions than I was to what she was actually doing. I hissed in shock when she ripped the current bandage off in one quick swipe.

"Gah! You just jumped right in there, didn't you? Sheesh." My breathing was a bit ragged. I swear she just ripped half my skin off. Why did females wax?

Without her earlier tenderness, she wiped all the dry blood off my side. "Suck it up, buttercup. You want to be some big bad warrior, act like it."

Eric covered his mouth to hide his laughter from behind her. I scowled at him, and he stopped hiding it. I flipped him off.

"Told you she was a firecracker."

Well, at least he got that right about her.

Cassie replaced the dirty bandage with a clean one. Eric and I both watched as she moved around the room. My wolf growled in my head when Eric walked up behind her at the basin and put his arms around her.

Cassie didn't respond to him at all.

"Are you okay? I know it's been a weird day." Eric whispered to her, but I could still hear it. Thank you, wolf senses.

"I'm fine, Eric." Cassie tried to step away, but Eric growled softly and held her in place.

"Talk to me, Cas."

"Not now, Eric." She growled right back at him, hers sounding more tired and exasperated. "I. Just. Need. More. Time."

Eric roughly released her, forcing her to catch her footing. "Fine. I'll check on you both later."

I waited until he was gone, and I heard his footsteps move down the hall. "Does he always pout like that when he doesn't get his way?"

Cassie let out this odd annoyed, frustrated, snarky sigh. I had to laugh.

"All the freaking time. It didn't bother me as much before. Lately though, it bugs the hell out of me. Is it new?"

I shook my head with a sad laugh. "Sadly, no. I just didn't know he still did it. I love my brother, but he can be a big baby if he doesn't get his way."

"Yeh." She clicked her tongue as she came back over to sit down.

Before she could, I reached over and pulled the chair closer to the head of the bed. She smiled and shook her head but didn't argue.

"I have only seen him do it a few times before, but lately, it has been happening more often. I noticed the more I put my foot down, the more he complains and pouts." As she sat down, her hand reached for mine.

My wolf and I both swelled with pride. She wouldn't let him touch her, but she let us.

We talked about anything and everything over the next two hours. Some of this I had already heard from Eric, he talked more than the elderly females in the pack. Hearing it from her though, was worth so much more. My mate was so much more than I ever would have thought.

How are you feeling, Ricky? My father linked in.

I put up a finger for Cassie, not wanting her to think I was ignoring her.

Better. Cassie says it is healing, just slowly because of the wolfsbane.

Good to hear, son. How are the two of you?

Nearly perfect. Pretty sure I would heal faster if I could hold her.

I could hear his silent laughter. *We always do. Why don't you?*

Eric. She is worried about him coming in. She doesn't want to hurt him.

I think we can all appreciate that. Anyway, your mother says dinner is ready. Do you think you can walk now, or do I need to make up an excuse for you two to stay hidden in that room?

I smiled. I loved my dad.

"Dad wants to know if I am well enough to go down for dinner. Or…" I played with her fingers still in my hand. "We could claim I can't walk and stay here longer."

She shook her head and smacked my hand. "Tell him we will be down in a few minutes."

Well, it was worth a shot. We'll be down soon.

Roger that.

Cassie pulled back the corner of the bandage, then the rest of the way off.

"Not bleeding anymore at least. I suggest you shift after dinner. It should help finish the healing process."

I swung my legs over the side of the bed and sat up. I probably could have been up sooner. I just enjoyed having her waiting on me. We hadn't heard from Eric since he came in, hours ago. I was slightly curious as to how my parents kept him away from Cassie and me.

Cassie stood close by, ready to help me if I needed it. I let her think I did. As soon as I was standing, I pulled her to me and laid one on her. I didn't hear any complaints from her, so I wasn't planning to apologize.

"Thank you for taking care of me."

She laid her head on my chest for a brief moment, hugging me close. "That's supposed to be my job."

She pulled away too soon and began to gather up all the supplies she had used. I grimaced at the sight of all the bloodied towels. I guess I bled more than I thought I had.

I wanted to question her use of the word "supposed," but I didn't want to bring up the lovely triangle we found ourselves in.

I walked over to where she stood next to the door and tried to take the tray from her. She just laughed and shook her head.

"Nope, I will carry this. You will carry yourself."

I let my wolf speak with a low growl, we wanted to help our mate. She laughed again and opened the door. I followed her carefully down the stairs and headed to the kitchen.

Dinner was awkward, and that was putting it mildly. My parents had held off long enough with the third-degree concerning Nate and why he had been there. Dad had already called Allen and they got it all cleaned up.

If it had involved humans, we would have had to jump through more hoops legal wise. Since it didn't, most of it was going to be swept under the proverbial rug.

There really was no way to handle it when "broken neck by a large wolf" was not listed as a reason for the cause of death. As far as we were concerned, Nate died in the line of fire. He shot at a cop, he lost. Case closed.

All people that would be involved legally, from the DA to his parents, were all wolves. No one was going to question anything.

The hardest part of dinner was Eric sitting next to Cassie. I sat across and one over from her, as far away from him as I could get. It would be too tempting to break his arm every time he put it over her shoulders.

After our few hours alone, Cassie had been relaxed and laughing. With Eric back in the picture, she was stressed and tense. And there wasn't anything I could do about it.

Once dinner was done, and the dishes cleaned up, Cassie insisted I shift. My parents went up to bed, but Eric said he would sit on the patio with Cassie while I ran for a bit.

I wanted to run with her. My wolf wanted to be with his mate again. I was sure neither of those things were going to happen tonight.

CHAPTER 16

Cassie

Eric sat down on one of the patio chairs, positioning another close to him for me. I had enough of the touchy-feely stuff through dinner. I lost track of how many times I told him to back off and to give me space, and then he ignored it.

Ricky gave me a speculative look as he took off for the trees. I knew he was worried, and he was uncomfortable leaving me alone with Eric.

Frankly, so was I.

Was it bad to say that I was glad Ricky had been poisoned? It gave us a chance to be together, just us. A chance to get to know one another a little bit. I let him hold onto my hand, that was it.

Not once did he push for more. The only time he kissed me was when he got up.

From day one, Eric had pushed for more. I was getting to the point where I didn't trust his wolf. I didn't trust him.

I still didn't want to hurt him though. I still didn't want to cause a rift between the two brothers. I still didn't know what to do.

"Cas. Come sit down. Talk to me. I feel like I've hardly seen you since we got here."

I kept my eyes on the stars, not wanting to look at him, and not wanting him to see me watching for Ricky. Logically, I knew he was fine. Emotionally, not so much.

"I've been sitting most of the day, Eric. I don't want to sit."

"Okay." He drew it out, almost like it was a question. Then he stood up and wrapped his arms around me from behind.

I closed my eyes and took a breath. "Eric. What happened to giving me space? We decided in the car that it would be better for your wolf if we took a few steps back. You haven't done that."

Instead of backing away, like he should have, he lowered his head to press it against my cheek. He actually laughed, a small breathless laugh, but still a laugh.

"I'm not sure I'm physically capable of being near you and not touching you."

I scowled into the air. "Are you physically capable of listening to me and giving me what I want?" I snapped.

He jerked back, like I slapped him. Finally releasing me. He leaned against the rail in front of us, just off to my side, his arms folded across his chest.

"What the hell is going on, Cas? Ever since we got here you've been closed off and moving away from me."

I knew him well enough that I could hear the hurt in his voice, the hurt that I was causing.

I lowered my head to look at the rail, my hands grasping it as I leaned on my arms.

"I just... I'm trying to figure some things out. I keep trying to tell you that I need space to think, and you aren't giving it to me. I feel like you are ignoring what I want, Eric. It's always about what you want."

Eric lifted his hand to the opposite side of my face that he was on and turned me to look at him. "Hey," he kept his voice low, like he was talking to a scared child. "I thought we wanted the same things. I know I can be selfish at times. I know that. I'm trying to work on it." He gave me a sad, sarcastic smile. "I left you alone to take care of my brother, didn't I? *I* wanted to hover over both of you. For different reasons of course. I left. I'm sorry I'm making you feel this way. I don't mean to be. It just feels natural to be touching you and to hold you. It's what we've always done. I just need you to talk to me and help me out here."

Dang he made some good points. I laid my head on his shoulder, he, thankfully, didn't push for more than just that.

"What's wrong, Cas? I can't help fix it if you don't talk to me."

From a distance, I could see Ricky starting to make his way back. I quickly lifted my head and stepped away from Eric.

"I'm going to bed. It's been a long day."

Ricky's wolf heard me as well and turned his head. The thing about fated mates, no matter how long you'd known each other, you had this innate ability to read every little detail about them. Including the smallest changes in their voice that gave away how we were really feeling. And that was before the mating, where the real connection was made. Before he would have an all-access pass to my feelings and thoughts.

I spun on my heels ignoring the "I love you" coming from Eric.

I sprinted up the stairs, and straight to my room. I fell asleep arguing with myself on whether I wished I had never come, moved to Washington, or glad I at least got to meet my fated mate because of all of it. I couldn't even fully wish I hadn't met Eric. I wondered if a part of me would always love him?

CHAPTER 17

Ricky

It always felt good to shift after an injury. It was like walking again after being stuck in a chair for hours on end. There would be a slight soreness in the muscle, but after that, you didn't ever want to sit again.

Even though we didn't want to go far from Cassie, we also didn't want to hear or see whatever was going to happen on that patio. Normally my wolf would push for more time, more speed, more distance. Tonight, it was the opposite. Even he was anxious to get back to her.

They didn't look like they had been fighting. Yet, she still sounded distraught. Enough so that even Eric caught it. His face wasn't much better than hers. What the hell did they talk about? Did she break the news to him finally?

Eric stood to walk inside after Cassie. I was close enough by that point, I barely had to raise my voice.

"Leave her."

Eric froze in the doorway, his whole body slouched as he turned around and sat down.

"You're right."

I froze as I pulled my shirt over my head. "Care to say that again, give me a chance to record it. I'll need it for proof when you argue that you never said this."

He huffed, leaned back in his chair, and lifted one leg onto the small wooden table.

I was going to hate myself for this in the morning. I sat down next to him.

"Wanna talk about it?"

Eric gave me the "are you serious?" side eye. He shook his head. "I guess I should be happy that at least someone wants to talk to me. I'm starting to think we shouldn't have come home."

Her yes, him, eh… maybe. That was debatable at the moment.

"She still not talking to you?"

"Yes and no. She called me out on my selfishness. I know, that's not new. I am trying though, Rick. I'm trying to put her feelings first. I'm trying to keep in mind that what she wants matters."

Progress, at least he was trying for one person.

"I just… I thought we wanted the same things. It always seemed like it before."

Man, now I was feeling guilty for finding my own mate. Why did it have to be the one person who got my brother trying to be a better person? Why did we have to fall for the same female?

I cleared my throat uncomfortably. "What's her biggest concern? Let's start there."

Eric rubbed his hand over his face, scratching his jaw as he went down.

"She keeps saying to give her space. I... uh," he huffed, "can't seem to stop touching her all the time. She's right though. I did agree to take a step back after my wolf lost control the other day. In retrospect, I may not have been totally in agreement, just placating her. She seemed fine, I guess I didn't realize how not fine she was. I didn't think she would actually stick with it."

I should feel guilty for what I was about to do, but I honestly didn't.

"Then you need to back off and give her space. Stop touching her all the time." The grimace slipped out. He laughed.

"Is it really that bad?"

I glared at him. He had no idea. "You might as well have been humping her leg during dinner."

He got a good, embarrassed, laugh out of that. "I'm glad you two are getting along, and she feels comfortable enough to talk to you. What did you guys do up there all day?"

I shrugged, trying not to look at him. It was a good thing the sun had already gone now. He couldn't see the guilt in my eyes.

"Nothing, we just talked."

"Talked about what?"

"Quit fishing." I snapped at him. "I'm not telling you anything. She will tell you when she is ready."

He frowned. "Did she at least tell you what she meant when she said no one else was dying to protect her?"

I licked my lips and pushed them together. His head dropped to the back of his chair.

"Yeah. I figured. Any chance you are going to tell me?"

"Nope. Her story to tell. Not mine."

"I get it. You're honorable, you don't betray people, not even just a bit by sharing something personal."

If it wasn't for how laid back he was right now, or the fact that Eric had never been good at keeping his feelings to himself, I would think that was an intentional barb. He wasn't like that though. He didn't dance around anything. He was a "tell it like it is" kind of guy.

I still felt it though. I wasn't trying to betray my brother. In fact, that was why she was keeping her distance from me too. Because she didn't want to hurt him. Or me.

"I had planned to ask her to marry me in a few days." He turned and gave me a sardonic smile. "Think that would be considered pushing it?"

I laughed at his unveiled idiocy. I lifted my thumb and forefinger, holding them millimeters apart. "Just a little bit." I even raised the pitch of my voice.

We talked for a bit longer, reminding me how much I did miss my big brother. All his faults included. If Cassie wasn't my mate, I would be happy for him and take a more active approach in trying to help him fix things.

Then again, if she wasn't my mate, there wouldn't be as much to fix.

We eventually made our way back inside. I was wiped after hardly any sleep, then getting shot, and dealing with finding my mate.

We were both opening our respective bedroom doors when we heard the crying. It wasn't loud enough for my parents to hear it on their floor, but it was loud enough for us to hear it in the hall.

Both our heads snapped up. Eric half ran to get to Cassie's door, he had barely passed me when he stopped suddenly.

"I want to go in there and comfort her." He turned to face me; his face filled with pain. "But... I also know what she sleeps in. I showed up early the other morning, she wasn't ready yet... I... I don't know if he can handle this. What do I do, Ricky?"

"You just did it." I closed my door again and stepped between him and her door. "You thought of what she needed, not what you needed. You also recognized your weakness. I'll go. Just a warning, your wolf may not like seeing me comfort her in her bed."

He nodded once and started walking backward, back down the hall.

"Thank you." His voice was hoarse and dry. His whole demeanor shouted that he was in pain.

Growing pains. They sucked.

I waited until he was back in his room, then carefully went inside hers. Cassie's head was moving back and forth, she was mumbling and crying in her sleep.

"Katie, no!" It wasn't loud, Eric probably couldn't even hear it. But I heard it with every cell in my body.

I hustled over to her bed, grateful I hadn't worn shoes outside to shift, and climbed on the bed with her. I carefully slid Cas into my arms and held her close. I began shushing her and rubbing my hand down her moonbeam hair.

A few moments later, she took a deep breath, pulling my scent in. Her body shivered and then relaxed. She never woke up, but my presence soothed her enough that the nightmare was over, and she was able to sleep peacefully.

I debated getting up.

I decided against it. I would just tell Eric I fell asleep.

It wasn't a lie. I really did fall asleep, faster than I had expected to as well.

CHAPTER 18

Cassie

It had to have been the weirdest night of my life. Exhaustion claimed me quickly, thankfully, but it landed me in Alaska, fifteen years ago. Next thing I knew, I was surrounded by Ricky's scent. I remembered nothing after that. I slept so deep, I didn't dream. Not that I could remember anyway.

In fact, the scent was so strong, it felt like he was in the room with me. Even though I was awake, I held my eyes closed. I didn't want to risk ruining the serenity I was feeling. It was much better than the turmoil I felt on a regular basis lately.

I suggest you open our eyes and let us revel in this.

If I open my eyes it will all go away.

No, it won't. She sounded so smug it made me curious.

I opened one eye slowly. I was met with dark blue. Strange. I opened my other eye and looked closely.

I was a little ashamed of how long it took me to realize it was a t-shirt. The very same one Ricky put on before dinner.

Am I seeing things?

My wolf sighed. *No. He heard us crying last night in our sleep. He came to comfort us. He is a good mate.*

Hmmm. Yes, he is.

I took advantage of the opportunity given to me and snuggled in closer, like a pup to its mother on a cold night. The arms I hadn't noticed before tightened their hold on me, and the blue shirt vibrated with a very deep hum. His breathing was still slow and steady.

Is he awake? I questioned my wolf, no matter the form, she had better control of our senses than I did.

She gave me a wolfish giggle. *No. That's his wolf. He's awake. Ricky is not.*

Huh, cool. Just out of curiosity. I rubbed my head against his chest, the way his wolf did to me when we first met in the woods. I pressed my lips to hold back my own giggles as the playful growl vibrated through him harder.

Now you did it.

What?

I felt Ricky shifting under my head, so I tilted it up. *Oops.*

He shook his head, a tired smile on his lips.

"Are you playing with my wolf?"

I shrugged. And then laughed as Ricky found my ticklish spot on the first try. It was hard to bite my tongue, not wanting anyone else to know we were awake. He didn't go for more than a minute, thankfully. It had been a losing battle against the noise.

I took a couple steadying breaths. "Thank you for coming to me."

His furry, unshaven, morning face tickled as he kissed my forehead. "That's my job. I'll always be here to take care of you."

I didn't miss how he basically repeated my words, just not verbatim. I didn't know how I was going to tell him I had to leave. I couldn't be with either of them without hurting one of them. I couldn't get in the way of their family dynamics.

Feeling a little panicked, I swiftly looked towards the door.

"He knows I'm here."

My eyes widened as I looked back at him. Say what now? He smirked down at me, lifting his hand to graze his knuckles along my cheek.

"It was his idea, actually. We were just coming upstairs for bed when we heard you crying. Eric started running over but stopped before opening the door. He didn't trust himself or his wolf enough to come to you. I warned him not to come check on us at all, his wolf wouldn't like it."

"You stayed longer though. He's going to know. He's going to be mad. I don't want you two to fight." My breath started racing. I never should have opened my eyes.

Ricky shrugged. "Eh. I was tired. I fell asleep. Yesterday was a *very* long day for me. I did get shot."

I rolled my eyes at him. "You were grazed." I poked him in his stomach, hard enough to make him flinch.

He paid me back by pinching my butt. We both realized immediately that it had been a bad choice. My body had jumped away from his grabby fingers and further into his hard body. When my eyes met his, I could see the fiery blaze of desire burning as bright as mine.

His voice was hoarser now than it had been when it was just filled with sleep. "We should probably get up."

"Yeah." My voice was the opposite of his - high pitched, like the squeak of a mouse.

And… neither of us moved an inch. Well, I didn't, and he didn't in my view. Certain things he didn't have as much control over, certainly did.

"Cassie. I'm going to need you to stay very still while I get off this bed."

My eyes creased at the serious tone his voice took. "Ricky? What's wrong?"

"Nothing, love. My wolf is feeling a little frisky right now. He doesn't want to hurt you. If you move, he might accidentally start chasing you. We don't want that. So, I am going to move first. You need to to stay right here until I am gone. Promise?"

The frown came unbidden to my face. Which he didn't like. He braced his forehead to the top of mine and breathed deeply.

"It won't always be like this, I promise."

Yes, it will. I whispered in my head. I held back the tears and nodded once.

He pressed his lips together, seeing through me, like always. He kissed my forehead forcefully, holding it for three seconds. Yes, I counted. Then he was gone. He practically ran out the door.

Why can't we stay with him? My wolf whimpered.

You know what Yolanda said. Eric was planning on proposing on Christmas. Tomorrow is Christmas Eve. I don't know if he is doing it then or waiting for Christmas morning. It's not fair to lead him on like this. The longer this goes on, the more everyone will be hurt. Do you really want to hurt him? He was going to be our chosen mate. If not him, then it would be Ricky hurting.

We will hurt them both by leaving.

I know. But at least they will still have each other.

I pulled myself out of the bed and climbed into the shower. Once I was done, I began repacking some of my things.

How are we leaving?

I don't know the answer to that either. I guess I could always call an Uber.

And what about school? Eric will track us down there.

I stopped packing and looked out the window. It really was beautiful here. It may not have been long, but I knew I was going to miss this place.

I think it's time to go home.

My mind was empty of words, but our emotions were filling the space just fine. She may have been upset with Eric, but that didn't change the fact that she had once chosen him too.

I took three deep breaths before walking out the door. Yesterday, Eric had been waiting for me. Today, he wasn't. No one was in the hall. Huh. That made me feel… relieved, obviously.

But also, a little sad.

I heard laughing coming from the kitchen and followed the sound. This wasn't the biggest pack house I had seen, not that I'd seen many, but it was still larger than a normal house. I smiled, confused, when I walked into the kitchen. The only person missing was Ricky.

Eric jumped out of his seat and came around. He sweetly kissed my head and picked up my hand. He didn't try to hold me, he kept space between us.

"Good morning, beautiful. Hope you're hungry. Mom always makes too many pancakes."

I laughed. "I didn't think that was possible. Not with how much you and Ricky eat."

His parents laughed again. Eric started to pinch my waist but stopped and pulled his hand away.

He's finally giving us space. The man who chose to love us, of his own free will, is trying to give us what we wanted. My wolf was shocked and torn.

That is not helping any!

I know. And he is not helping me. Being mad at him made all this easier.

Welcome to the land of confusion. Population now two. The weather sucks, the view sucks. Everything about this place sucks.

"Here you go, Cassie." Bea set a plate down on the table and I forced myself to walk over to it.

I cautiously sat down to eat. Eric sat next to me but kept his arm off my chair.

"Did you sleep alright?"

I nodded as I chewed the bite I had just put in my mouth. I've always been curious to know why people *always* asked you a question right as you took a bite of food. Did they want us to answer them with food falling out of our mouths?

I covered my mouth as I swallowed. "Fine. Why?"

"I could hear you crying in your sleep."

Right, that. "I guess I had a bad dream. I really don't remember any of it." Eric looked confused. He also didn't look like he believed me. "These are really good, Bea. Thank you."

His parents looked uncomfortable. I could only imagine what all this tension must feel like from the outside.

My wolf sighed. *I envy them.*

Me too.

"Did I hear mom made pancakes? Awesome! I'm starving." Ricky practically shouted with glee as he came through the door.

Eric rolled his eyes and appeared to relax. They started joking around, teasing each other about who eats more. They had such an easy relationship.

And we were ruining it.

I... I... I tried to talk to my wolf, but I couldn't even push the thoughts past the lump.

Go, just go now. Who cares what they say. Let's just get out of here.

I stood up from my seat so fast, Eric had to grab my chair to keep it from toppling over. Ricky's eyes met mine. He read my distress and closed his eyes. I took off.

Sometimes I wished I didn't have such good hearing.

"What happened? What'd I miss?" Eric said, before I even hit the stairs.

"Stay Eric. Let me talk to her. Sometimes we just need to talk to another female."

I heard softer footsteps following me. I didn't bother closing the door. I just went straight to the bed and collapsed on the pillow that Ricky had laid on, letting his scent wash through me. I vaguely heard the door close behind me and then felt a soft hand on my head. Which made me miss my mom.

Me too. Let's go home.

It was like I had just been waiting for my wolf's permission. I jumped back up, startling Bea and grabbed the last of my things.

"Sweetheart, what is going on? Why are you packing?"

"Because I can't stay. I've ruined your family by leaving Alaska. I never wanted to do that."

Bea stood up and grabbed my hands, my toothbrush and toothpaste still in them. She pulled me back to the bed and sat us down. With one hand she pushed my hair behind my ear.

"Oh, sweet girl, that's not true. Who told you that?"

I sniffled and looked away toward the window. "Nobody had to tell me. I just know."

"Talk to me, what happened? Is it because of Nate yesterday? That had nothing to do with you."

I snorted. "Yes, it did."

She gave a small incredulous laugh. "Honey, Nate has always had his issues. He was mad at Ricky. He would have come after him one way or the other."

I shook my head vehemently, my hair flying everywhere. "Ricky didn't tell you the whole story. Nate wanted Ricky to feel what it was like to lose a mate."

"But.." Bea flounder, probably thinking I was making no sense. "Ricky hasn't met his mate yet."

I sniffed again. *This crying bit is really getting old. We've cried more in the last few days than we have in the last few years.*

"Yes, he did."

She gasped, pulling her hands away. She was going to hate me for this. "What? When? Why didn't he tell me?"

"Two nights ago, the night we arrived. He went for that run after work… I… I just needed to get some air. There was this smell driving my wolf crazy." I finally let my eyes meet hers, begging for her to understand that I didn't come between her only two sons on purpose.

It took her all of ten seconds before she gasped again and covered her open mouth. I shrank into myself, falling into a ball on the bed.

"Is he your fated?"

"Yes." My voice was whimpering and weak. Not my proudest moment.

"I take it you haven't told Eric, yet?" She was managing to keep her voice steady and calm, like none of this was a big deal.

"I love both of your sons, Bea. In very different ways. Both of them want me to be their mate. One of which is not very good with rejection. No matter what I choose, I will be hurting someone. As soon as Eric finds out…" I chickened out, I couldn't say it.

She sighed. She already knew the rest. He was going to go ballistic. "Tell me everything that I have missed."

I rolled to my back and told her everything. And I did mean everything. I even told her about Eric losing control of his wolf. She was a patient listener. I was going to miss not being able to spend more time with her.

"And then, the way they were joking around just now. I couldn't take it. I don't want to be responsible for ruining that. I don't know any way to fix this without repercussions. All I can think is that if I leave, at least they will still have each other."

"Yes and no. I know my boys. I guarantee it will all come out. But…" she sighed dramatically. "If you are not here, if they both lost you, then eventually they will commiserate together. A mom can hope anyway." She gave me a very sad and depressing smile. "I'm sorry that it has come to this. You are a good fit for our family. It's nice to see a female keep my male pups on their toes."

I sat up, wiping the last of my tears away. "Do Ubers come out this far? The sooner I go the better. Before the bond with Ricky is too strong. I need to know that he can still move on. They can both find a chosen, preferably *separate* females this time."

Bea scoffed both in disbelief and amusement. I didn't want to ask what she meant by it. I was so done with talking about all this. And I was still going to have to explain it all to my parents and my very overprotective big brother.

I wouldn't tell them about Eric's wolf losing control in the dorm room. That would not go over well with any of them, especially Pat. That was the plan anyway. Apparently my brain had a hole in it when I was upset, and Pat always knew how to get things out of me.

"Not that I know of. Doesn't matter. I will take you myself. Those boys won't put up as much of a fight if it's me."

"Thank you, for everything. And I am really sorry that it's come to this."

She wrapped her arms around my shoulders and kissed the side of my head. "You did nothing wrong. Fate just likes to make things difficult from time to time." She leaned back and patted my cheek. "Don't fret. Everything will work out just fine."

I nodded, not wanting to argue. Let her keep her positive thoughts. They didn't exist for me anymore.

Bea picked up my duffle bag and I picked up my backpack. She led the way back downstairs. She was able to make it to the car unhindered. I was not. She must have mind-linked her husband because he was waiting at the bottom of the stairs.

He pulled me in for a hug and whispered in my ear. "It will work out. It may not seem like it right now, but Fate does know what she is doing. Don't give up."

"Cas? What's going on? Why do you have your bags?"

Eric. Guess I knew I wasn't going to be able to leave without saying something.

I pushed my way past him. He was shocked enough that he didn't stop me. He managed to pull himself out of it right as I made it to the doorway. He stopped me with a not so gentle hand on my arm.

"Why are you leaving? Your flight isn't for three more days. Did something happen to your family?"

I turned my head away from him, which of course was the direction to where Ricky was standing near his police cruiser, in full uniform. If I had waited five more minutes, I would have missed him. I didn't know if that was a good thing or not.

"Because my choice will tear apart your family. I love you both, one more than the other. I can't bear to hurt either of you. Goodbye, Eric."

With all the control I could muster, I pulled my arm out from his grasp and headed for the car. Eric was so shocked and confused, he stayed where he was, just watching me.

Ricky didn't have that problem.

He grabbed the car door as soon as I opened it. His whispers were practically wind, keeping them between us... and Bea who could no doubt hear us from the driver's seat.

"You don't have to do this. You don't have to leave, Cas." His voice cracked, revealing how much I was hurting him.

"I don't want to leave you. I don't know what else to do though, Ricky."

"Stay with me. Please." His eyes filled with water along with mine, both of us felt like someone was tearing our souls in two again. Fated mates were not meant to leave each other. "I need you."

I groaned and sniffled again, my hand was itching to reach out and touch his cheek one more time. I raised my eyes and saw that Eric was still standing in the doorway. Lost, hurt, completely confused.

There was also a slight bit of hope in his eyes that his brother would be able to convince me to stay. From Eric's point of view, we probably just seemed to have created a good connection over the last few days. It made him proud that I got along so well with his family.

When I met Ricky's gaze again, I didn't have to explain any further. It wasn't like we hadn't talked about this before. Many, many times.

I shook my head sadly. These would be the last words I ever said to him. "I'm truly sorry, Ricky. For what it's worth, I do love you. Very, very much. Enough so that I can't come between you two. I can't live with the thought of you losing your brother, your best friend, because of me. Find someone who will make you happy, someone who won't ruin everything."

Ricky dropped his head and groaned. That was not going to be easy for him. Ricky never wanted a chosen mate. He only ever wanted his fated one. Me. But we could never be. Not unless Eric were to magically meet his fated mate. That was doubtful, seeing as he only had a few months until he was due to take over as Alpha.

Even if he chose another, it wouldn't erase his feelings for me. Only the power of fate could do that.

We managed to keep the entire conversation between us. If Eric heard anything, it would have been lost with the wind, making it indecipherable. Bea though was a different story. She was sitting behind the wheel crying.

I slid into the car, placing my backpack at my feet. Ricky closed the door, his eyes never leaving mine. Bea was working to stifle the sobs as she pulled out of the driveway. Her heart must have been breaking right along with mine.

During the car ride, where the only sounds were hiccups and a background of some random music station, I looked up flights on my phone. I would have a three hour wait, but at least I would make it. Bea dropped me off in front of the airport twenty minutes later, after a very emotional farewell.

I steadied my breath and walked inside. I waited in line to get my boarding pass. The line was so long, long enough that I could make another call.

"Hey, little sister. What's going on?" Pat sounded happy. I was glad he was happy.

I hiccupped and that was all he needed.

"What happened?" He didn't sound so happy anymore.

I looked around at all the people. Maybe calling him right here hadn't been such a good idea.

"I'm coming home early."

"Okay...what time does your flight get in? I'll come pick you up."

"I don't really know yet. Probably tomorrow. I'm flying to Seattle first so I can pack everything else up. I'll let you know what time my flight is for tomorrow."

If he wasn't happy before. He *really* wasn't happy now. "Cassandra? Why are you packing up your dorm?"

I took a deep breath again, straightening my back. "Because I'm coming home, Pat. I'm in a crowded airport right now, not really the place for me to get into it all."

I could hear the wheels turning in his head. I could even picture him pinching the bridge of his nose, his eyes closed tightly, and the small but firm frown that would be under his large hand.

"I'll meet you at your dorm. We will talk there."

"What? No! Pat, you don't have to do that!"

"Yes. I do. Please, Cassie? Let me help you."

"Thank you." My voice cracked with gratitude this time.

"I'll see you tonight. Message me your dorm info."

I nodded, even though he couldn't see me. "Okay."

The wait was torturous. I tried to read books on my phone, but I couldn't focus. I settled for texting Yolanda and letting her know I was leaving.

Me: Do me a favor, wait until New Year's to tell Jordan. I'm going home.
Yolanda: like, home-home, or back to the dorm home?
Me: home-home.

Yolanda: *sad face* I'll miss you.
Yolanda: sorry it went all wonky.
Me: I'll miss you too. You can have whatever I leave behind. I can't take it all back on the plane.
Yolanda: I'll hold onto it in case you decide to come back.

If only I could.

Me: Whatever helps you sleep at night, babe.
Me: boarding now. TTYL
Yolanda: fly safe. Call me!
Me: Will do.

I checked the time, but still had another hour to go. I only felt slightly guilty for lying to her. I had too much other guilt rolling through me to feel too bad about it.

CHAPTER 19

Eric

I spent the entire day after Cassie left, trying to figure out what went wrong. No way this was all from just that one incident. She was relaxed at breakfast. Ricky and I were laughing. Then suddenly she couldn't get out of the room fast enough.

Ricky kicked a few tires after she left, then sped off to work like he was Dale Earnhardt. I thought for sure he would get her to stay, or at least him stay and tell me what she said!

Why couldn't she talk to me the way she talked to him? How was it in a matter of days, he knew more about my girlfriend than I did?

My parents were no help either. When I turned to my dad, he only had one thing to say.

"It's not my business to tell, so don't ask. And don't ask your mother either. Leave her be."

"So, basically everyone knows what the hell is going on but me?" I couldn't believe this.

My father gave me that look, the one that said I needed to rethink my attitude and remember who I was talking to.

"Sorry." I deflated quickly. "I'm just confused, dad. I have no idea what's been going on lately. I thought I figured it out, and now she's gone, before I could even try and fix it!"

I collapsed onto the couch, folding my arms and pouting. Probably looking like a dang pup. I fixed my face fast. This wasn't about me. It was about Cassie. Something happened that made her pull away. She obviously needed more space than I was capable of.

My father sat down on the couch next to me and put a hand on my shoulder. He waited until I looked at him before he spoke.

"You are just like I was at that age. Pig headed and stubborn. I didn't like being left out of things. I didn't like it when things didn't go my way. You are in a tough spot, Eric. I think you are finally waking up to some of the things you need to work on."

I frowned. Things? As in, more than one? I had more than one thing I needed to work on?

My Alpha father thought that was quite funny. He patted my shoulder a few more times before squeezing it as he stood.

"Just keep in mind that not everything is about you. And sometimes, we have to sacrifice for the ones we love. It's the hardest part of growing up." He left after dropping those confusing words of supposed wisdom. Words that made no sense and told me nothing.

Mom took longer than I expected for just a trip to the airport. I had the feeling she was avoiding me. On the other hand, it may not have had anything to do with me.

Wow, I really was a selfish prick.

I hid in my room the rest of the day, trying and failing to figure it all out. I called and texted Cassie, frequently. She never responded. She didn't even read them.

I never heard Ricky come in. The one person I knew was on my side. The one person I knew would talk to me. Maybe now he would break her confidence since she wasn't here anymore. If it helped me fix things, she would forgive him. I think.

I emerged from my cave and searched through the house. His cruiser was out front, so where was he?

I walked towards the back and heard the sound of glass bottles hitting each other. Sure enough, there he was. Sitting on the patio.

Drinking a beer? Since when did Ricky drink?

I wasn't exactly going for stealth as I joined him, in the same seats we were in last night. I waited, but he just ignored me, as though I wasn't even there. Alrighty then.

"Thank you for trying to talk her into staying."

Ricky answered me with a grunt. Screw the man card, screw being polite.

"Do you know why she left? I did what you said. I gave her space. I hardly touched her all morning! I even stayed clear of her room when she was obviously very upset." I pushed my hand through my hair and gripped it like I was going to pull it out. "And what was all that crap she said about loving someone else? Did she say anything to you about that? I haven't heard or seen her with anyone else… ever! Please, brother? I need your help!"

Ricky huffed in annoyance and anger. "Oh, yeah. I know *everything*." The way he drew out the last word had my back up. That made it sound like there was a whole lot that I was missing.

My head snapped back to him. How could he know so much more than me? Would he really finally tell me?

"What??? Wh… why did she tell you and not me? We've been together for months! Why the hell did she talk to you and not me? Whose furry behind do I need to beat?" I nearly jumped out of my chair.

Ricky huffed again and took a slow drink of the bottle he was holding. It was obviously not his first for the night, there were two empty bottles rolling around next to his chair. And from the full ones next to those, it would not be his last.

"Why is my girlfriend leaving leading you to drink? Something you never do." There was no way she was talking about Ricky. No. As hard as I tried not to go down that road of thought, my voice was still full of suspicions.

My brother gave a deep, dark chuckle. One that I never would have believed had come from him if I hadn't been sitting right next to him.

"You don't want to hear it, trust me. That's why she left after all, to protect your sensitive little heart." Ricky polished off the bottle, set it down and picked up another.

With a quick swipe, he used the rail of our patio to pop the top off.

Who was this male? This was not my brother.

Ask him. I don't want to believe it either, but we need to know.

I opened and closed my fists, trying to not let my wolf take over again. Through my teeth, I did as my wolf wished.

"Did you mess around with my *mate*?" I made sure to emphasize mate, hoping to stress the serious betrayal that would have been.

Just as everything else has gone today, Ricky did not react the way I expected.

Ricky threw himself out of his chair and threw the open bottle against the rail, the liquid flying with the glass as it shattered across the patio, us, and the grass.

He growled at me, his wolf wanting to come out and play. "Your mate? Yours? Right, because everything is about you. She came because of you, she left because of you. All because you can't just wait and look for your fated mate like the rest of us. And once again, I get screwed out of something I want because the "future Alpha" called dibs." He even used mimed quotation marks.

I was stumped by both his words and his behavior. Right before my eyes, I saw my brother lose control of his wolf. Even as a pup, when his wolf first emerged, he rarely lost control. Maybe twice in his entire life did it happen. And here he was, 23 years old, shifting without taking his clothes off, then taking off into the woods.

Now, I knew I was selfish, but I was working on it. Slowly yes, but it was a work in progress. However, I would *never* be selfish enough to take someone's fated mate! Cassie told me herself that she had not met her fated. It was rare for her pack. So why the hell was Ricky throwing it in my face?

Did he think that was some kind of excuse to mess with my girlfriend? The one I chose to be my mate?

I stripped - I really liked this shirt - and shifted, following after him. He was not going to run and hide from me. I was tired of the no answer answers everyone was giving me. But this, no, this concerned me. He was going to tell me what I needed to know.

I followed him for miles, always at least a hundred feet behind him. Sheesh he got fast. When was the last time I ran with my brother?

Not the point. We need to catch him, make him talk. Find out what he did to our mate!

I felt my wolf put a burst of speed on and then skidded to a stop. Ricky was slowing down, his whole body shaking as he entered a clearing I hadn't seen before. My wolf and I slowed down and walked toward him as he sniffed the ground and then collapsed.

A small part of me worried about my brother, the larger part though was feeling too betrayed to care too much about his feelings. I stalked over and loomed down on him. I was his future Alpha. He would not defy me.

Ricky didn't even budge. Once again, acting like I wasn't even there.

Why, Ricky? You have always been my best friend. You're my brother, for crying out loud! Why would you go and try something with my mate! I began pacing back and forth. Then, froze as the wind softened. *Why is there a faint scent of Cassie here?* It was days old, but I could find her scent anywhere.

Ricky's thoughts floated back to me. The tint of them was one of someone who no longer cared, like they had no reason to even live. That startled me as much as his next words did.

Because this was where she laid the other night. Staring at the stars. She said it reminded her of home, of her... family.

Cassie never mentioned being homesick. If it hadn't been for her comment about loving both of us, I would never have excused her hasty exit as anything more than a desire to see her family. Maybe with how close Ricky and I are... were... made her miss Pat?

Unfortunately, she did make that comment.

You were out here with her? You both snuck around behind my back? Cassie wouldn't betray me like that. Would she?

This is where I met my mate. My fated mate. She was more than I ever imagined. Her wolf ran, and mine caught her. It was perfect. And then it wasn't.

Ricky's thoughts were melancholy, bringing light to the deep depression he felt. I laid down next to him, my nose pointed at him, wanting to find a way to comfort him. Feeling relief that I was wrong, a little guilty for assuming the worst, but mostly I felt for my brother. I knew how badly he had always wanted to find his fated mate.

I'm sorry, brother. Cassie is a great listener. I didn't realize she was helping you through that. Why didn't you tell me?

Ricky's large head turned away from mine, making what I thought was supposed to be a scoff of disgust. I waited. He didn't answer.

Had I been too caught up in my own world to know he needed me?

I thought back over all our recent conversations. We only ever talked about Cassie. If I had palms at the moment, I would have slapped my head.

I never gave him a chance to tell me. It was always about me. Dad was right, there were many things I needed to work on. Starting now. I was going to be a better brother.

When did you meet her? You should have called me.

My question was once again met with nothing but silence. Well, not complete silence. Ricky's breathing was heavy and stunted, as though he was trying hard not to cry. Which was yet another thing I had never seen him do. With the tip of my nose, I nudged my baby brother. Even my wolf was feeling guilty.

Please man, talk to me. Let me help. Cassie just left me. I think I can understand better than anyone how you're feeling right now.

For some reason, that made Ricky laugh, hard. The mixed laugh of the sad, mad, ironic variety. Which just confused me more. A state I should just start getting used to at this rate. Worrying about others, getting their opinions, trying to do their will instead of mine... it was all really confusing.

You really want to know big brother? You really want to know why I lost my fated mate and you lost your chosen mate?

Yes! I am tired of all these secrets already!

Ricky shifted back to his human side, pushing himself to a sitting position, folding his legs in front of him. I quickly followed suit.

"The night you and Cassie got here I came home late."

I gave him the "yeah, I already knew that" nod. None of us would forget the after effects of that night. Nate's actions affected all of us. Not even 24 hours passed before I thought I was watching my only brother die right in front of my eyes.

Ricky just shook his head at me, rolling his eyes.

"I was already agitated because of Nate. I was exhausted. All I wanted was to go home and pass out. But there was this smell, I tried to figure out where it was coming from. It was perfect. It sang to my soul, it called to my wolf. I couldn't find the owner of it though. I planned to give mom the third degree in the morning, see who she had over. The smell was everywhere, even my room, my wolf was restless. So, I went for a run. I had barely shifted when I caught the scent again, this time leading to the woods. I followed it, and sure enough, it led straight to her. She was laying right here, watching the stars."

Ricky's eyes closed, a serene smile crossing his lips. I felt a little lighter, joy for my brother. Then his smile faded, fast, and I remembered this story ended with my brother depressed and angry.

Ricky swallowed a lump growing in his throat. "Her wolf was beautiful, her fur shone in the moonlight. It was almost like she had been born from it. She was fast. We had to work hard to catch her. It was worth it though. That was the most fun we ever had playing with someone. Eventually, I had her pinned. Then she shifted. As soon as I was furless again, I kissed her. It was… it was like a piece I hadn't known was missing had been put back in place. My wolf was urging me to mate her right then and there. But she pulled away, like she just remembered where she was. She started crying and took off again. She kept whispering no and shaking her head for me not to follow."

"Why though? Why did she run? Did you get her name at least?" I would help him hunt her down if I had too. I hated seeing him in so much pain.

Ricky shook his head sadly. "Not at that time, no. I hardly slept all night."

I waited, as patiently as I could, but he did not continue. I was dying inside. I needed to know. Even if I couldn't fix things with Cassie, maybe I could at least fix things for him.

I wasn't used to practicing patience, it was really hard.

Ricky growled and stood up, pacing away from me. We had shifted around each other so many times, nudity wasn't an issue. It was common in packs, even more so when you were close in age to your brother. When you were first learning to control your wolf, everyone got an eyeful on a regular basis.

I forced myself to stay seated, knowing he would tell me eventually. Ricky just needed to get it all off his chest, and at his own pace. With his back still to me, I finally got my answer. To more than just one question.

"I saw her the next morning… at breakfast."

I didn't remember seeing anyone else around the pack house for the last few days. Mom made sure we would have privacy, so my family could have time to get to know Cassie.

I was thinking hard, trying to remember if someone had stopped by for even a split second. I nearly jumped when Ricky gave this deep groan, growl type noise. Shouting it out into the sky. Wherever my memory was lacking, his was not.

I listened carefully as his voice was deceptively softer than his body language and his previous noises of frustration and pain.

"I was so excited when I smelled her again. It was so fresh, so strong, I knew she was still there. She had to be somewhere in the house. And I was going to find her, even if I had to look in every dusty corner. I followed it, down the stairs... straight to the kitchen." He swallowed hard, looking right at me, "straight to *your* arms."

I tilted my head, not understanding what he was talking about. My arms had only been around Cassie for half a year. Yeah, it took me longer than I was proud of to catch up to what he was saying.

I closed my eyes, focusing on what happened that morning. I mind-linked him to get down there. I wanted to see him. A few minutes later, Cassie shivered and then tensed... when she saw Ricky. That was when she began pulling away from me, at that very moment. She even tried to push out of my arms.

No, she had been distant that whole morning, it just increased when she saw Ricky.

My head fell into my hands. It wasn't what happened before we left. It was what happened while I slept, and they were out here. The key thing I had been missing all along.

I didn't want to say it, but I did anyway. All while my wolf whimpered.

"Cassie is your fated mate. That's the choice she was worried would tear apart our family." My breathing increased as I thought over all of her words as she had left me, the words that were etched into my heart. "She was going to choose you. She loved you more."

The last words were barely out of my mouth when Ricky shifted back into his wolf form and howled pitifully at the moon. Every shifted wolf in the vicinity felt his pain and sent out their comforting howls.

Ricky took off again, this time I let him leave. I had my own pain to deal with.

I lost my love, someone I planned on spending the rest of my life with, all because of my brother. But I was also the reason why my brother wasn't going to have his fated mate. The one female he had always been waiting for.

I sat there, not so much for the silence, just not knowing what to do or where to go.

How could this have happened? How did we not know? My wolf was as distraught as I was.

I don't know. This explains a lot though.

My wolf flashed the memories of the way she screamed for him when he got shot, the way she hovered and refused to let someone else take care of him. The way she watched for him after he shifted again.

Are we so blind to everyone else that we missed it?

Eventually, I made it back to my room. I sat on the edge of my bed the rest of the night, not even bothering to try and sleep. I listened, worried about Ricky. I waited, but I never heard him come in.

I guess I was making progress. Even though I was mad at him, and fate, I still worried about him.

I met my parents for breakfast, which was a subdued affair. I didn't even touch the eggs and bacon my mother gave me.

"Where's Ricky?" My father asked. "He's not responding to me."

That was concerning, yes. "I don't know. He took off last night." My voice sounded dead, even to my own ears. I was never going to get her back now.

I only looked up when my mother sniffled. My eyes creased when I saw the red tint and the bags under her eyes. Looked like I wasn't the only one who couldn't sleep last night.

"I knew that was his howl." She whispered.

I nodded.

"You know then. He told you?" My father sounded just as morose as the rest of us.

"Yes." My response was clipped. I didn't care if it was disrespectful. It seemed as though I was the only one who didn't know they were fated.

My mother started sobbing again right before she ran out of the room. Much in the way Cassie had. Right after she saw Ricky and I laughing. Man, I was such a blind moron.

"And?" My father pushed for more. It wasn't a push I wanted.

"And what?" I snapped. "And the woman I love, fell in love with my brother. All because fate told them too. This, right here," I stabbed the table with my finger as I leaned forward, "this is why I don't agree with fated mates. Cassie and I were perfectly happy together until fate stuck its big nose into things."

The front door slammed, and Ricky walked into the room. "Really? You really think you were perfectly happy? What happened the morning you came here, right before you left? How often did you push for what you wanted, ignoring what she wanted? How often did she confide in you?"

I stood up, letting the chair fall to the ground. "That was one time, something that would never happen again and was only a problem because we were ready to make it official. Until she saw you anyway!"

Ricky scoffed and half turned, then stopped. A small sarcastic smile, one that said he knew something I didn't.

"If things were so perfect. Answer one question for me. Whose Katie?"

I opened my mouth to answer... and then stopped. I opened it a few times, thinking I had it. His grin grew every time. It was a trick. She wasn't real.

"You made up a name to prove your point."

He shook his head, smiling. As though he were disappointed and yet not surprised.

"I'll tell you. It will answer the question I refused to give you the day I got shot. Katie *was* Pat's twin sister. Cassie's *older* sister. I'm sure you remember when she got upset with you when you teased her about Yolanda acting like an older sister?" He paused for dramatic effect and then moved on.

"I'm sure you also remember, when I got shot, Cas was yelling about not letting someone else die for her. See. When she was five, rogues attacked. She was outside. Alone. Her brother and sister, only three years older, came out to protect her. Katie saved her life that day." He licked his lips. I noticed the small tremor in his voice. "Katie paid with her own life."

All three of us had to take a second and breathe. "So, you see, dear brother, if things had been so perfect, why didn't she tell you about that?"

"Why would she tell you and not me?" Yeah, I heard the whine too.

"I asked her."

"So did I!"

"But did you ask her because it was information you didn't have that you thought you deserved? Or did you ask her because you generally cared and wanted to know her?"

"Same thing. I wanted to know everything about Cassie. I deserved to know everything about the mate I chose."

My father stood up, shaking his head sadly. "No, son. Learning things like that is a privilege, not a right. I have been mated to your mother for thirty years. I am still earning the right to share her thoughts to learn more about her. You can't take your mate for granted. And they always know. They know everything, even before the bond. It's a gift only given to the females, of any species."

Ricky and I were both huffing and puffing, like we had just run a race.

"But..."

My father cut me off with a small shake, he wasn't done.

"We will not discuss the subject of Cassie again in this house, not until you two can do it calmly. She left because she didn't want to cause a rift between you. She didn't want to ruin the close relationship that you have. She was trying to save you both." He began to walk out but stopped and turned to face me.

"Eric, I want you to think about something before you return to school. When you found Cassie, what was it that made you want her? Besides her beauty. Did you want her because of her laugh, because of heart? Were you entranced by her every time you saw her? Or... did you see a beautiful female that you wouldn't mind being your mate? Were you on the hunt for a chosen mate, desperate to prove that a chosen one was just as good as a fated? Did Cassie just fit the mold that you had created for her? Or at least she would once you were done helping her learn to fit inside it?"

My dad patted Ricky's back as he passed him, trying to give him some of his strength. Ricky and I stood silently staring at each other, until he turned and stalked out of the room as well.

The next week passed slowly and quietly. Hardly anyone spoke to each other.

Christmas morning was hard. I held the ring I had picked out for Cassie, as I sat in my room and allowed the tears to fall.

My wolf and I had many long talks, going over what everyone said. Cassie, my father, even Ricky.

My brother had always been the quieter one. But that was nothing compared to his silence now. Which spoke louder to me than anything else.

The original plan was to return to school a week after New Year's. I returned on New Year's day. There was too much tension in the pack house, and I was tired of the avoidance game between my brother and me.

I was also hoping to try and talk to Cassie as soon as she got back to school. I needed to talk this out with her. I needed her to help me understand. There was a small part of me that was hoping my brother was wrong, that all of this had been a really big misunderstanding.

A fool's hope to be sure, but it was still hope. All this felt like a bad dream I just couldn't wake up from. I needed my mate to straighten it out, to help me.

Through the whole break, I kept trying to call her and text her, I left her many messages. All still went unread. She gave no sign she even saw or heard them.

Until she blocked me.

When I pulled into the house. I was surprised to see Jordan waiting on the front porch. He and Yolanda had moved into their place the other day. My father had called and told Alpha Turner that I was headed back early. My new roommate was ready now and would be coming shortly.

Seeing Jordan waiting for me like that had me worried that something had happened. I sniffed the air, checking to see who else was here. I noticed that his scent was now blended harmoniously with his mate's scent. They must have finally made their mating official.

I grinned at him, happy for my friend. "Congratulations, man." I grasped his hand and pulled him in for a hug. His side of things was not as exuberant as I was expecting.

I could tell by the look on his face that something was, in fact, wrong. I grabbed my own bag and led the way inside the house.

"What's going on?" I threw my bag on the living room floor and sat down on the couch.

"Cassie's been talking to Yolanda for weeks. She didn't tell me anything until last night. When I got your message you were headed back, I figured I'd come check on you."

Jordan sat in the chair across from me, staring me down. His obvious worry wore me down. I had been fighting it for too long. I wasn't sure what the difference was with him knowing versus my family. Possibly it was because he didn't know my brother. He was *my* friend.

First it was one sob that broke free, then the rest came pouring out of me like a freaking waterfall after a hurricane. I couldn't remember the last time I cried like that. After a few minutes, I was able to pull the Alpha male back out of me and pull myself together.

"What happened? None of this is making sense to me." Jordan sounded generally concerned and confused.

I huffed. "Tell me about it. I'm still trying to figure all of it out myself. Most of it was kept from me until recently. I thought she was mad at me because of something that happened before we left. My wolf...we both were struggling...he took over. Cassie's wolf had to intervene before it was too late. I let her have space because I was feeling guilty. It wasn't easy, and she had to keep reminding me to back off sometimes. I let her leave, thinking it was because of me. I knew she had been talking to Ricky, I thought he was trying to help her."

I thought he was on my side. He was my brother. He should have been on my side. And everyone said that I was the selfish one of the family?

"I finally got it all out of my brother the night she left. As much as I want to beg him to help me understand, he won't talk to me and I'm not really sure I want to talk to him either."

Jordan shook his head with a soft chuckle. "Yup, still need some context here, bud,"

I groaned a painful sigh and leaned back, sinking into the couch.

"From what Ricky told me, Cassie and he are fated mates. I only know his side of things. She basically pushed us both away most of the time. But there were times when they were alone and were able to talk. He kept finding ways, and she didn't fight *him*." I sniffed and gave a sardonic laugh. "I didn't even know what was going on. I thought she was nervous about being with my family. I had no idea she was torn on what to do. Now, my brother who has always waited for his fated mate, never going near any other female, has lost her. I've lost the female I chose, the one I love. And Cassie has lost us both."

"Yolanda said Cassie didn't want to come between you and your brother. That's why she left."

I nodded. "That's what both my mother, my father, and my brother have told me. Cassie only vaguely mentioned it when she left." I laughed sarcastically again. "I'm in such a messed-up place. I want to comfort my brother and help him get his female back. But I want my female back too! I don't know, but I think she fell in love with him. I think it was stronger than what she had for me." Jordan flinched and looked down. Hell. "She told Yolanda that, didn't she?"

He shook his head. "I don't know. All I can tell you is that there is no pull stronger than the fate bond. I had females in the pack that I had dated on and off before. Some I really liked too. That was nothing compared to the moment I first saw Yolanda, even just scenting her. For Cassie to fight it for so long, she must have really loved you, man. Ricky's wolf would have been pushing him to be near her at any chance. For him to hold back his wolf, especially when you would be trying to hold her… he loves you a lot too. It's a sucky situation for each of you."

I rubbed both my hands up and down my face.

"What are you going to do now?"

"I'm hoping if I corner her on campus somewhere, maybe go see her at work, she will have to talk to me."

I may not have been directly looking at him, but Jordan was still in my line of sight. He shifted uncomfortably in his chair, not meeting my intense gaze again.

"Jordan? What do I not know?" I asked him carefully, dreading any other shoes dropping on my head.

He looked like it was causing him pain to answer, like I was pulling his teeth out to get it.

Jordan scratched the small cropping of hair growing out on his chin. "Yolanda promised Cassie to not tell me until New Year's. She probably knew that I would tell you as soon as I found out. I promise Eric. I would have told you sooner had I known."

My breath increased. That did not sound good. "What did she promise not to say?" It was barely even a whisper, but he heard me anyway.

With a deep, regretful sigh. He dropped the largest shoe of all, directly on my head.

"Cassie didn't fly straight to Alaska. She came here first. Her brother showed up that night, helped her pack her things up and they left. She's gone, Eric."

And the last bit of floor I had been standing on just fell right out from under me. I should have claimed her months ago when I had her in my bed. None of this would have happened. Their bond would have disappeared before they even met.

The only thought worse than that, was the small inkling of guilt, knowing I still would have kept Ricky's mate from him. He would have kept going on, looking for her, when she was no longer there, for his entire life.

CHAPTER 20

Cassie

The holidays were one big blur to me.

Pat showed up on my doorstep, hours after I got home. As Yolanda was still at her parent's house, I let him sleep in her bed. I felt like I held it together pretty good, up until he stepped inside. Then I crumbled. He just held me until I cried myself to sleep.

The next morning, I woke up and promised myself that I would not cry anymore. I made a choice, and it was time for me to stick with it. I had to keep reminding myself that the black hole that once was called my heart, was worth it. Ricky and Eric needed each other, they were brothers first, and best friends second.

What's that saying humans used? Bro's before ho's? That was all this was.

By that night, Pat and I were back in our parent's home. They were there, waiting for us. Once we had everything back in my old room, I hid myself inside and left Pat to explain the situation to them.

It should have been a happy holiday break. While I had been gone to school, Pat finally asked Stacey out, and they were doing great. They were really cute together. Which made it even harder to watch.

So many questions ran through my head though.

Was that how Eric and I once looked? Was that how Ricky and I would be right now? How it could have been, had Eric not already been in love with me?

And the biggest questions…

Where were their fated mates? What if they were to meet them now? Would my brother be as broken-hearted as me? Probably not. Stacey only had brothers.

And finally…why did they get the happy ending, and I didn't? Did I have a past life that I royally screwed up to the point that fate and karma ganged up on me to torture me in this life too?

When New Year's passed, I called the University and told them there had been a family emergency. After lengthy discussions with all of my professors, I was able to finish my classes online.

Which was perfect for me, I had no desire to be around people at the moment. Humans and shifters alike. My family rarely asked how I was anymore, they settled for looks of concern.

My Luna came to visit. She and the Alpha had been informed of my return. My mother was kind enough to explain what happened. If I was capable of infusing my speech with sarcasm, that would have been sarcastic. Unfortunately, in order to keep a lid on my depressed emotions, I had to cap them all off.

A few days before the term started again, Yolanda called. We had messaged back and forth every few days. She hinted that her and Jordan had officially mated, but because of my melancholy mood, she kept the celebration away from me.

On some level, the guilt for that was there too.

She explained to me everything Jordan told her. Which was all told to him by Eric. I probably could have heard it straight from Eric, but I blocked him around the fiftieth phone call. I refused to read his messages too. He wasn't who I wanted to talk to.

It wasn't until around Valentine's Day that it fully sank in. I left because I didn't want to come between the brothers. I did anyway. Ricky told him.

If that was the case, then... why hadn't Ricky tried to call me?

Did he already find someone else? I wanted him to. Hell, I told him to! *I* left *him* after all. Now that he could actually look for a chosen, surely there were more than a dozen females lining up outside his station waiting for him.

By March, I came to the conclusion that Ricky hated me for leaving him. A dominant male like him, that had to have been a low blow.

With the end of the term came Summer vacation. I no longer had anything to keep my mind occupied. It was also time for me to decide what I wanted. I never did get around to doing my volunteer hours. The idea of going near a patient just reminded me of helping Ricky.

"Knock, knock." Pat called as he knocked and opened my bedroom door without waiting for my response.

I was sitting in a chair, looking out my window. Something I did frequently.

"Cas?"

When was the last time I heard anyone call my name without worry?

I cleared my throat, pasted on the best fake impression of a smile I could, and turned to him. It must have been bad because Pat grimaced.

"Listen, I have an idea. Something I hope will help you." He paused awkwardly. I waved my hand for him to continue. He cleared his throat. "Right. Anyway, I decided to continue my residency in California. With our cousins. The hospital near the Mojave pack lands has offered me a position. I was thinking… you should come with me."

I creased my eyes, not quite understanding why. We used to visit with our relatives every year, typically during winter break when it wasn't so hot. Our mother's brother was the Gamma there. He often brought his female pups for a visit during the summer.

Pat, knowing I wasn't quite following him, continued. "You need females your own age. You always had fun with Lauren and Tasha." He sighed with frustration, looking around my room with his hands out wide. "This is not living, Cas. It's not healthy. You need to get out, you need to change things." He lowered his hands back down to his waist.

"Stacey will be coming as well, as my mate. I'd really like for you to come and stay with us, or with Uncle Cameron. I've already spoken to him. They would love to have you. You can stay as long as you like. As long as you need. Stacey and I will be there for the next two years, at least."

I swallowed. "You asked Stacey to be your mate?"

He hadn't told me anything about them, ever.

He smiled shyly, my brother's true personality, as he blushed. "Yes. We are going to have a little ceremony before we leave. Will you come to the ceremony and California?"

I nodded as I stood, walking over to my big brother, giving him a hug. "Congratulations. And, yes, I will come. To both." Not like I had anything going on here. Maybe a change of scenery would help.

The ceremony was held during the first week of June. We left for California two days later.

Pat was right, being with my cousins was helpful. Lauren, the oldest by two years, had been lucky, her fated mate was in their pack. They grew up together. Tasha, who was my age, had not yet met hers. She didn't seem to mind though. She enjoyed the attention of all the males, both shifter and human.

Tasha was the crazy one of the bunch, she had no patience for my depression. They both spent the first night asking me 1001 questions. Then, they literally pulled me out of the house and to the gym.

Their pack didn't often train females; however, they would work out with me when they visited Alaska, and then bugged their father for official training. It felt so good to move again. Within a few days, I began feeling more like myself.

Pat had been right. This was the best place for me to finally begin to heal.

CHAPTER 21

Ricky

I sighed with relief when Eric went back to school early. The tension in the pack house drastically cut down. My parents still walked on eggshells around me. Which really wasn't helping.

I managed to get up and go to work every day. I may have also been a little rougher with suspects and moron drunks than I normally would have been. Needless to say, my patience was at an all-time low.

By the time Spring hit, I was moving into my own place. It wasn't much, just a small cottage deep in the woods. The place was small, completely surrounded by trees. The backyard was really a small clearing. Plenty of room to put in a fire pit, some lawn chairs, and room to lay about, looking at the stars, in either form.

My wolf and I spent many nights watching the moonbeams hit the grass. In our mind's eye, we could picture our perfect mate lying out in the grass.

In the beginning of July, my father called a meeting with his Beta, Gamma, Eric, myself, and Travis. The old leaders who would be retiring and the new leaders who would be coming in. We had a little less than two months before Eric turned 25 and neither of us had our mates.

"At the end of this month is the yearly regional conference. This year, it is being held on the Mojave pack lands. As per usual, I will be leaving Beta Michael and Travis in charge of the pack while the rest of you come with me."

"Father," Eric spoke up carefully, more reserved than I had ever heard him speak before. "What if Ricky and I haven't mated in two months? Are you sure that we should be going and not someone else? Maybe Travis should start planning, give the others a heads up."

I huffed. It wasn't my fault I hadn't mated yet. But I followed the warning in my father's eyes and kept my mouth shut.

"No. We will continue along as though you two will be stepping up. We still have two more months. A lot can happen in two months."

There was a small twinkle in my father's eye, as though he knew something we didn't. It was gone just as suddenly as it had appeared. Must have been a trick of the light.

Over the next few weeks, my father insisted on the three of us, Travis, Eric, and myself, training together, working together, and eating together. I was surprised he didn't have us sleeping together too.

My first impression when we disembarked the plane in Las Vegas was that it was way too hot. Then, when we got out of the car in Mojave, I immediately missed the heat of Vegas. It felt like someone had sucked the air right out of me. Along with every ounce of moisture my body had previously.

"Gah! Can you imagine living in this?" Kent, one of the pack warriors who traveled with us, grumbled in my ear.

"Never. Not even in my worst nightmare. How can anyone survive in this heat?"

Kent shook his head and pulled out his bottle of water. He poured a small amount on the dirt path. We both watched in horror as the water dried up within seconds.

Before we could continue lamenting and whining, our hosts for the week stepped out of the pack house.

It wasn't a large pack house, but it was spacious. Thankfully they had an air conditioner running. Even with that though, it was still too dang hot.

We spent the next three days in meetings and touring the pack lands. This was normal. In Europe, the shifters had a regional council. Wolf shifters that oversaw the packs. In America, we preferred to be free.

The Alphas and Gammas from each pack in a region met once a year. The Alphas were in charge of the whole pack, like a president. The Gammas were the head of security; therefore, they were the Alpha's number one bodyguard.

In the Alpha's absence, the Beta, like a vice-president, was in charge of the pack.

Typically, the Alpha position was handed down to the eldest son. However, if another child was more dominant, then they could take over. Also, if someone in the pack believed they were the best choice for the job, they were welcome to challenge the Alpha in a fight to the death. While that was rare, it did happen on occasion.

We rotated who hosted the conference of Alphas, that way no one Alpha was set above the others. It also gave each pack a chance to show off a bit. We discussed what happened during the previous year, what changes we were looking into making, introduced the incoming leadership, and saw who needed help with what.

This year, our pack was the only one with a shift in leadership. Alpha Roger had much to show off though. Over the last two years, with the help of their pack doctor, Dr. Kostas, they had renovated their pack hospital.

As was often the case these days, their hospital catered to both humans and shifters. We walked around the grounds, looking at all of their new equipment and their new wings.

I only half listened, I was back to thinking about Cassie and wondering if she decided what she wanted to do yet. I was a fan of the idea of her being a nurse.

Cassie had such a soft touch and was easy to talk to. It wasn't that I didn't think she would be a great doctor, she was the smartest wolf I knew. But Cassie had a big heart. She would want to spend time getting to know her patients. Comforting them when they felt alone. She would never be able to move on after only five minutes of talking to them.

On the fourth day, we split up. Alphas went one way, while Gammas went another. Gamma Cameron, the Mojave pack Gamma, took our group to their training center. This was their chance to show off the fighting prowess of their warriors.

It was also a great time for the males to have rematches from past years.

The fights could get pretty brutal, so I wasn't surprised to see they had a first aid station set up near the side door. Nor was I surprised to see that it was being manned by a doctor and not a paramedic.

Something about the male seemed familiar. I couldn't put a finger, or a paw, on how I knew him though, or who he was. After a few confused minutes, I shook it off and focused on the two old timers in the fighting ring.

A young pup walked in and handed something to the doctor, drawing my attention once again. This time, it was drawn by the breeze passing through the door, pushing the male's scent toward me.

He carried two scents. One scent was obviously his and his mate's, the perfectly blended scent they created. The second did not belong to either of them. This was one he got from being in recent contact with someone else.

A scent that I would know anywhere, no matter how much time had passed.

I quietly sauntered over to him, monitoring every step, making sure my wolf was in check. I was going to have to play this very carefully. I half expected my wolf to jump out at any minute and go on the hunt, after biting this male's head off.

Oddly, he was calm but felt just as confused as I was. We really hadn't spoken much since Cas left. We were both barely surviving, just going about our daily routine. Well, I'd been going about my daily routine. He spent most of his time curled in a ball in the back of my mind. It was a step up from the regular cursing out he gave me in the beginning.

"I'm going to try and make this sound as non-threatening as possible, even though my wolf wants the opposite." Not really, but normally he would. Not that this male needed to know that.

"Alright…" He gave me the briefest of looks before turning back to the fight, watching carefully in case he was needed.

I watched the others as well, keeping my voice low so we wouldn't be overheard.

"Why do I smell my mate on you?" Despite my desire to keep the threat out, and his original aloofness, my wolf added a growl at the end.

Look who was finally waking up.

The male was confused and turned to look at me. "I have no idea. Is your mate visiting with you? Was she in the hospital recently?"

I shook my head. "I have no clue where she is. I haven't seen her in months."

He studied my face carefully, probably trying to put the pieces together. "What pack are you from?"

I lifted an eyebrow, not sure what that had to do with anything. "Glacier. Why?"

The male closed his eyes and leaned back against the wall with a defeated sigh. "Ricky, or Eric?"

"Why?" I growled again. That time I let the threat roll.

"Because I'm not telling you anything until I know which brother you are."

The male leveled me with a look of his own, not caring that I was more dominant and threatening him. That shouldn't be surprising. Doctors were generally safe, no one was allowed to attack a doctor.

After a moment of silence, I smiled. I recognized the look of protectiveness in his eyes. Everything fell into place.

He was a doctor, smelled like my mate, and was protective of her. That left only two options. He was too young to be Cassie's father, which really only left one other option.

"Ricky. And I'm guessing your Pat."

Pat smirked and raised his hand in greeting. I happily accepted it.

"Where is she? How is she?" My voice shook for the first time in months, at least in the presence of others.

Her scent on him is fresh. She's here. I bet anything she is here somewhere.

I know. And if we want any chance of seeing her again, we will need his help.

Pat cleared his throat and turned back to the fighters. "I'm going to be more honest than she'd probably like. Cas is an absolute wreck. She barely finished the semester, hardly left her room for months. I don't even remember the last time I saw her smile."

I groaned, my wolf accenting it with a whimper. A few of the others in the room turned to look. Gamma Allen lifted a questioning eye.

Are you alright?

Yes. This is Cassie's brother. She's here somewhere, I know she is.

Patience, Ricky.

Allen had become my confidant these last few months. My parents did their best, but they were stuck in the middle. Allen wasn't. He had no reason to play nice for Eric's sake. He never cared much for my spoiled older brother anyway.

"You have no idea how much I want to tell you where she is right now. She needs you." The sadness in his voice told me he was speaking the truth.

"She told you everything then?"

"Yes." He shrugged sadly. "She always has. She may try to keep some things to herself at first, but eventually it all comes out."

I nodded, swallowing. I took a deep breath, willing my emotions to settle. I tried to pull out the careful facade I had been wearing in public since the night I got drunk and spilled everything to my brother. Well, the day after that anyway. I had no problem rubbing in his face how little he actually knew about her. That had actually felt *really* good.

I just had to keep reminding myself that I was in a room surrounded by warriors, which was not the best place to shed any tears.

"Did her leaving do any good?"

I huffed and snorted in the back of my throat. "No. All it did was make everyone miserable. I got drunk that night, a first for me by the way. Between her leaving and Eric pushing me for everything I knew, I exploded. He knows it all. Our pack house is like a graveyard. Even the pack members avoid it at all costs. They don't even know why. Eric has one month to find a mate, or our Beta takes over as Alpha. He's not even looking. Actually… I don't know if he's looking. We haven't spoken since the day after she left."

I didn't mention my need for one either. I could care less about being Gamma.

Pat wiped the lower half of his face with his hand, pulling his bottom lip out as he pulled his hand away.

"What will he do if he finds out she is here?"

I shook my head. "I have no idea. I'm struggling not to take off and hunt her down right now."

Pat scoffed and gave me an incredulous look. "Who says she's here?"

I chuckled at him. "Her scent is fresh on you. No more than an hour old."

"Right. Hunter. Almost forgot." Pat's eyes took on a blip of mischief. "I love my sister. However, I don't always agree with her choices…"

My curiosity peaked. My wolf begged for him to finish, but Pat had frozen as the door opened and his face changed to a sarcastic snarl. I sniffed the air and smelled my brother and the other Alphas coming in the gym.

I stifled the grin fighting to come out. "I take it you have issues with my brother."

Pat's eyes never wavered from the cocky prick that had just walked through the door. "As I said, Cas tells me everything. I had forgotten what he looked like until now."

"Did you meet him before?" That was news to me, I didn't recall either of them talking about Eric meeting anyone in her family.

"No, but she showed us pictures over Thanksgiving."

I hissed. She had pictures of him, but we never got to the point of having pictures together. I knew for a fact Eric didn't have any. It wasn't his style. It was mine though. I would have loved to have had pictures of her. They'd be all over my walls by now, allowing me to look at her beautiful smile every day and not rely on memory alone.

My father and brother walked over to us, both of them watching Pat warily. He wasn't exactly trying to hide his animosity toward Eric.

Something I need to know about, son?

Yes.

My father turned to me in surprise, obviously not expecting that answer.

This is Pat. Cassie's brother. Sniff him.

Ah. She's here then. I was hoping that would be the case. Good. It's time to end this.

Huh? Whatever, not the point right now. *What about Eric?*

He's grown. He will have to accept it and move on.

I nodded once and looked at Pat. "Call her."

Without removing his eyes from my confused brother, he asked, "Are you sure? I won't let her be hurt again."

"I will ensure she isn't. Call her."

He went silent for a few minutes, his face hardly giving anything away. When he finished he turned and walked over to the Mojave pack Gamma. He whispered in his ear, and the Gamma bent over laughing.

"Perfect. I love it. Thank you, Pat." What did he just do?

The Gamma gave the sparring pair a few more minutes, then clapped his hands, gaining everyone's attention.

"Gentlemen, if you wouldn't mind, shift back, and get dressed. We are about to have some company." The two wolf heads tilted in confusion then did as he asked. "Thank you. Now, in just a moment. I have three of our pack's strongest warriors coming in. They are not officially warriors, but they are fierce. And a force to be reckoned with."

A few of the local wolves groaned and stepped to the back, earning curious gazes from the rest of the males in the room.

"Not many packs insist on training members of their status, nor do they train them in human form. However, these warriors did not give us much of a choice. All three are cousins, two locals, one a temporary transplant."

I grinned and met Pat's eyes. I got it now. He told Cassie to bring them with her. And they were going to put on a little show.

"The locals kept spying on our training sessions. They had visited their cousin up North and saw others like them learning. They no longer wanted to be left out."

The double doors of the arena opened, and I nearly fell over from the fresh scent. It hit me with such force. My memory did not do it justice. My wolf shoved his way forward, wanting to get to our mate as soon as possible.

At the same time, Eric stiffened, his eyes flashing black. Lovely, this was going to be a nightmare.

"Gentlemen, let me introduce you to every rogue's worst nightmare. Lauren, Tasha, and Cassandra."

CHAPTER 22

Cassie

Cassie?

It's only been an hour. I am a big girl, Patrick. I don't need you to keep checking in on me like this.

My overbearing brother smirked through the link. *No, dear sister. I need you to come to the arena. There are some wolves here who need a lesson in humility. Bring Tasha and Lauren with you as well.*

I laughed, getting odd looks from our cousins. Okay, so I was still a work in progress. I laughed once in a while now, just not this joyfully.

It will be our pleasure to show them how it is done.

"Alright, females. How do you feel about showing a few warriors how it is done?"

My two favorite cousins cackled with glee and jumped to their feet.

Lauren rubbed her palms together and smacked her lips. "I do believe I am ready for my dessert."

"Yes, it's been ages since we served up some humble pie around here." Tasha added with a flick of her hair.

Lauren's mate, Lynn, rolled his eyes and stood up. He knew very well that she was going to be ripping her shirt off and fighting in her sports bra. No matter how many times he complained, she still did it. So, they compromised, he would stay nearby to make it clear to the others that she had a mate.

She was more than capable of taking care of herself, but she let him do it to keep him happy.

Being with them was helping me more than I thought it would. The down side, seeing how happy Lauren was with her mate.

We quickly changed into our workout gear, having been on the verge of leaving for a nearby mall, and made our way over to the arena, which was only about a block away from Lauren's house.

We stood outside, giggling as Uncle Cameron gave us our wonderful introduction. At the right moment, we opened the doors and stalked in, to a whole lot more males than we were expecting.

Instead of being nervous, it only made it better. The room stank of sweaty males. There was something else there though, something lying on the outer rim. It was sweet, but I couldn't quite lay my finger on it.

I strode further in, Gamma Cameron, my adoring uncle, was still talking.

"Gentlemen, let me introduce you to every rogue's worst nightmare. Lauren, Tasha, and Cassandra."

There were more than a few chuckles of disbelief, like they were hearing a great joke, floating around the room. My uncle always had been a bit of a show off, this was obviously what he wanted.

He shook his finger at the crowd as we made our way to him. "Don't underestimate these females. They will surprise you. I also will warn you. Two of them are my pups, the other belongs to my dear sister."

The warning was clear, mind your manners.

"Now. Miss Cassie hails all the way from Alaska." He held a hand out to help me through the ropes. I didn't need it, but I took it anyway. Something about his grip though felt more like he was offering a different kind of support.

"Don't let her size fool you. Every female is trained to fight in that pack, and not just in wolf form either. Do I have any volunteers?"

A deep voice called out from the side. A voice I never thought to hear again. A voice that had my wolf jumping out.

"Me. She's *mine*."

No one could miss the possessive quality that took over his voice, nor the double layer of tone. It wasn't just the human side speaking. I was being verbally claimed in front of everyone.

Why did you do this to me, Pat?

It needed to be done.

I will get revenge on you for this later.

He chuckled, which I heard both in my head and outside of it. *I will gladly accept it, little sister. You need your mate.*

My uncle winked when he saw the flash of silver in my eyes. He lowered his voice enough so that I would be the only one to hear him.

"Show him who the boss is, Cassie. Stop fighting it."

I nodded once and blinked the tears away as Ricky stepped into the ring. I rubbed my lips together and worked to steady my breathing. He grinned when he saw my eyes. His eyes answered with a glowing yellow.

Mate!

Yes, but make him earn it again. Remember, he didn't come for us. He didn't chase us. All these months, and not a word from him. Yolanda told us Eric knew everything. Why didn't Ricky come for us?

My wolf growled in my head. Perfect. I knew she just needed a reminder of why we should fight him.

We deserve a strong mate. If he is such a warrior. I will make him prove it!

That's my wolf.

I flashed Ricky a wicked grin, daring him to come and get me. I took one step back, which he took as his invitation to charge.

CHAPTER 23

Ricky

Don't go easy on them. I know it's our mate, but we need to prove why they belong with us. I instructed my wolf, knowing all he wanted was to pounce. So did I. Cassie looked really good in that outfit. It was also obvious she had lost weight while we were apart.

I will get our mate back. Look at the small female challenging us. She looks like a pup rebelling against their superiors. They step away, they know we are stronger.

No, they are taunting us. They want us to strike. They want us to chase. Do not get distracted.

He didn't listen. My wolf surged forward and charged. She was ready for that and danced out of the way.

"Tsk, tsk, tsk. Such a mighty warrior should know better." Yup, they were taunting us.

We growled.

Treat them like any other opponent. She wants us to prove our worth. So, prove it!

Cassie and I circled the arena, keeping a safe distance between us. I still worked my way closer, inching my feet every few steps in her direction. When I was close enough, she winked at me, then dropped to her hands and swept her right leg under both of mine.

I jumped, pulling my feet to my butt, just barely in time to miss it. I laughed as my feet hit the ground again.

Cassie was one step ahead of me though. While I was celebrating that small victory, she was already lifting her feet up again, all her weight on her hands, and double kicked me in the gut. As I fell on my butt, she dropped to hers and did a backflip, putting herself back on her feet.

Are you really going to let your mate beat you like this? In front of all these males?

I was startled by the sudden voice in my head. *Really, Eric? Now's the time you chose to talk to me again? When I am in the middle of a fight?*

Yes. You won't let me talk to you any other time.

I stood back up, threw him a scowl, and turned back to my mate, who was ridiculously pleased with herself right now. I almost smiled at her. She was gorgeous and she was a good fighter.

Make it quick then. I snapped at him. Irritated with both him and me. I needed to focus.

I just have one thing that needs to be said right now… Claim what's yours, little brother.

I froze mid-step, keeping Cassie in my sight. She tilted her head, concerned, knowing something was going on. She glanced to the side of the gym, her eyes widening when she saw Eric.

Thank you, brother. I wasn't going to question it. I was just going to go for it.

My wolf added a burst of speed as we flew across the rink at her. She turned, slightly startled, and swung. I lifted my hand up and caught it, turning her around, holding her arm locked behind her.

I lowered my head to her neck and took a long inhale of the unconcentrated version of her scent. It was strong, it was perfect. I heard the soft whimper coming from Cassie and kissed her neck. Her arm slackened so I loosened my grip.

I really should have known better.

As soon as my guard was down, she slammed her head backward, right into my jaw. Followed directly by her free elbow, into my ribs. Cassie stepped away, spun around, and lifted her knee up.

The room filled with groans from every male as I sank to the floor, first to my knees then to my back, with my knees curling into me.

Is that really the best you can do, little brother?

Shut up.

I rolled over, onto my hands and knees, and then pushed myself back up.

"Low blow, Cas."

"Bite me, Ricky."

I chuckled. "Is that an invitation, sweetheart?" We both ignored the snickers from around the room.

"At one time, sure. Now. No."

I drew my eyebrows together in confusion and stepped toward her. She took two steps back, still on guard.

She is angry at us? My wolf whimpered, saddened by the idea. *Why?*

I don't know. I was just as lost as him by her statement.

"What are you talking about? You're the one that left."

"I noticed that, yes. I also noticed that you didn't follow. Even after everything blew up."

I lifted an eyebrow and then dodged another kick, then a punch. She kept swinging, I blocked as many as I could. A few made it past my arms. She was moving fast enough that I was too busy trying to block her to throw one of my own. Not that I wanted to hit my mate.

She's fast. Our mate is a warrior. Perfect for us.

Not helping, bud.

"Oh yeah, I know what happened on your end. Yolanda told me everything." She threw her words at me with force, along with a fist that I barely missed by moving my head to the side.

Sorry, dude. I've been talking to Jordan. Who probably passed the message on.

I ignored my brother this time. "How was I supposed to know that you wanted me to come after you? You told me not to!"

She shook her head and started to turn away. I used that split second to grab her from behind again. This female was fast though and had more skill than I expected. I had barely grazed her skin before I found myself flying over her shoulder and landing on my back. All the air shot out of my lungs.

Our mate is strong.

Stop ogling her fighting skills and help me out here!

No. I told you we should chase. You said no.

I groaned. He was right. I did say no. It was one of the reasons he stopped talking to me. I pressed my hands next to my head and flipped myself up from my back.

"You knew why I left. Once it was all out, once you two had already stopped talking, there was no more point to any of it. You should have come. But you didn't!" Her voice cracked and she dropped to her hands again. This time succeeding in sliding my feet out from under me.

I stayed on my back this time. I acted like I was worn out, knowing she would come closer. She wouldn't be able to resist. Cassie didn't want to hurt me. She would feel the need to come check on me.

Sure enough, after a brief moment, she did. As soon as she got close enough, I kicked out and tried to knock her down. Her reflexes were faster than mine though. She jumped with plenty of time. A pair of female snickers were heard off in the distance.

I rolled to my stomach and started pushing up, then swiped my legs backward, kicking her in the stomach. Not hard, just enough to catch her off balance. Then swiped her legs out from under her. As soon as she was on the ground, I did what she should have done. I pinned her.

I held her arms above her head and sat on her thighs. I only used enough weight to keep her legs down. I was too heavy. It would have hurt her.

She kept her head turned, refusing to meet my eyes.

"Cas?" She studiously ignored me. I sighed, and then groaned as her bottom lip trembled. "I didn't think you wanted me to chase you. If I had known, I would have been on the first flight to Alaska. Ask any one in my pack. I've been a black hole without you. Baby, please."

After another moment of silence from her, I began to feel a little aggravated with the accusations. I growled softly.

"If you knew everything, you could have called too. The phone works both ways."

She sniffled but still didn't respond. During the fight, her wolf had backed off, her blue beginning to shine through again. From the corner, I could see the silver coming back. While her sky-blue eyes were a sight on their own, the silver, which nearly matched her platinum, moonbeam hair, was magic.

She turned to face me, finally, her wolf taking over. I wasn't sure if that was a good thing or not.

"You are the male. It is your job to chase." Cassie's voice was laced with the rough growl that was unmistakably a wolf speaking in human form.

"She said not to chase her."

"You are a warrior. Do you need a reason to fight? Your mate is enough reason. We were in a vulnerable position. There was no right answer. You did not fight hard enough."

I chuckled. "Look where you are. I think I've fought hard enough. I've got the bruises to prove it."

A very terrifying smile grew across her face, her silvery eyes shining like stars in the sky. "You think this was enough?"

I crooked a half grin at her. "You are the one pinned to the ground, sweetheart."

Two seconds later, I was the one pinned to the ground. I had barely registered the twist of her waist and hips, as she managed to roll us over, trapping me with one knee on my groin.

"Never take a female for granted. You underestimated us, you kept most of your weight off of us. Next time, be a real male. Be the warrior you are. Do what you know must be done."

She kneed me in the stomach, jumped up, slid through the ropes, and was out the door in less than a minute flat. Pat started to follow her, but she threw up a hand and a dirty look, stopping him in his tracks.

Gamma Cameron stepped into the rink and helped me up. "Pup, take it from an old, mated male. Get out there and fix this mess. It's gone on long enough."

"Yes, sir." Didn't need to tell me twice.

I slid out of the ropes and chased my mate. As I should have done six months ago.

CHAPTER 24

Cassie

Where are we going? My wolf asked, confused by my sudden change.

Testing him one more time. We both screwed up. And I'm tired of everyone knowing our business.

I made it to a patch of trees and quickly stripped before shifting. The trees were not as abundant here as they were back home, or any of our recent homes. Nor was there very much grass, it was all rocks and dirt. It worked in a pinch though.

The local wolves were closer in relationship to desert wolves. They could survive out here. Not me, I needed the woods. I needed the water. I needed moisture in the air.

And when he catches us? What then?

Then we claim our mate.

Finally.

You would think she would have yelled it out, sighed it, something that would show emotion. But no. She just stated it like a fact. If I could see her face, I was sure it would have been deadpanned.

The sun was beginning to set as I found my spot. The place I had been coming to the last few weeks. There was shade, a small stream, and a great view of the stars.

I didn't bother getting comfortable, we had been able to hear Ricky since not long after we left. We stood near the water, my wolf dipping her muzzle into the stream, replenishing what we had sweated off. It was only a few moments later when he was joining me.

I waited to the side, as his wolf drank as well. My wolf shifted her weight, which probably looked funny. We were both nervous. We did just beat his non-furry side in front of two dozen warriors, and aired our dirty laundry to who knew how many pack leaders.

He followed us though. She found that to be more comforting than I did.

After he nearly drank the stream dry, not really but it sure felt like it, he turned his nozzle to us.

I wanted to be stubborn and glare at him. Unfortunately, I was not the one steering this shape. I could see how frustrated she must be with me on a regular basis.

My wolf lowered her head in submission. I mentally stomped my foot, scoffing, trying to demonstrate my disagreement with her.

Ricky stalked forward slowly. My wolf let out a low whimper as he got closer. He did look a little scary. Maybe she made the right call.

Was he ticked? He looked ticked. He should be. I left him.

Ricky didn't stop when he got directly in front of us, he kept moving forward. Until he was pushing his nose into the side of our neck. He rubbed back and forth until our wolf form relaxed, and we pressed our nose into him. We stood there for a time, our wolves doing their own version of a hug.

Ricky nudged me once, then began to shift. Soon, he stood in front of us, without a stitch of clothing on. Maybe this wasn't such a good idea after all.

"Come on, baby. Shift back for me, please?"

Nope, not happening. I know I said I wanted to do this, but that was before, when I was in the heat of the moment. Now, I was literally scared out of my skin.

Ricky lifted his hand and rubbed gently behind my ear. "Cassie, I can't talk to you in this form, yet."

My wolf's ears rose when he added the last word. *See, he still wants us. Talk to him! Please, Cassie. We need our mate.*

Gah! Fine. I kept my head turned away from him as we shifted back. Ricky's hand never left the side of our head, by the time I was human again it was cupping my cheek.

"Hey, beautiful. Please look at me. I miss looking into your eyes every day."

I huffed in annoyance. "It was two days, Ricky. You make it sound like months or years."

He quickly placed his other hand on my empty cheek and physically turned me to face him. With both hands on me, he stared earnestly into my eyes.

"Two hours, two days, two years, two decades. It doesn't matter how long it was. Living without you, even before I met you, was no life. I have no purpose without you. I have no reason to get up in the morning, to work, or even so much as breathe. I need you, Cassie."

A tear slid out of my eyes, and I sniffled. "Why didn't you call me?" Really that had been my biggest hang-up. I guess a big part of me hadn't thought he would really let me go. At least not for long.

Ricky's hands dropped, along with his head. His voice filled with the deepest pain. "You said goodbye, Cas. You said you were leaving. I didn't think I was allowed to chase you anymore."

"That's the trouble with males, they never think." My stab worked, he lifted his head and scowled at me playfully. I took a deep breath, needing to say one more thing first. "I thought it was because you were mad at me. That you hated me now, for giving up on us. That's why I didn't call you after you told Eric. I took your silence as your answer."

Ricky cursed under his breath then yanked me against his chest, wrapping his arms around my back.

"I hated Eric for being a selfish prick. I hated fate for the position it put us in. Most of all, I hated myself for letting you leave in the first place. Not once was I ever mad at you or hated you."

With one finger he lifted my chin up, his brown eyes meeting my blue ones. Our wolves had stepped back to let us work through the human side of the problems.

"I love you, Cassie. I should have said it before. I should have said it a thousand times since, no matter where you hid. I can't change the past, but I can promise to change the future. I will tell you every day how much I love you. If you'll let me."

I really liked the sound of that. "What about Eric? Will you two ever be able to make up? Will he lose being Alpha because of me?"

Ricky's thumb traced my bottom lip, sending a shiver through me, reminding me that neither of us were dressed.

He smirked at me. I forgot how much I loved that sexy smirk. "When I got distracted in the ring, it was because Eric chose that time to intrude into my head and tell me it would all be okay. What happens with the Alpha spot is his problem. You are my mate, that is all that matters. Fate gave you to me for a reason. Those two days were all I needed to know that you are my perfect match. You are who I was always meant to be with." He kissed my nose softly. "I love you, Cassandra."

I closed my eyes, feeling a rush of tranquility I hadn't felt in a long time. "I love you too, Ricky."

Having said all we needed too; Ricky pressed his lips to mine. It started with the softest of touches, and yet it felt like a log being thrown on the fire. It wasn't long before my arms were around his neck, one of his behind my head, and the other on my lower back.

Ricky slowly slid both hands down, grasping my own personal moon, and lifted me up. My legs wrapped around his waist of their own accord. He swallowed the low moan that slipped out of me, as we had new areas greeting each other.

Oh, so carefully, Ricky bent his knees and lowered us to the ground, laying me on my back. He finally broke our kiss, resting his head against mine.

"Tell me now if you aren't ready. My wolf and I need to claim you, but I won't do it until you are ready."

I smiled up at him. He was still trying to give me what I wanted. He always was good at putting me first.

Let me out. I'm ready.

Finally. I repeated her words from earlier, I failed with the flat voice portion though. Mine was a little bit more sassy.

Ricky growled in a very sexy way as the silver took over my eyes. They were immediately joined with his glowing yellow stars. Ricky started slowly, kissing down my neck and working his way down.

By the time his wolf made it to where he needed to be, ensuring his mate was ready and willing, I was practically hyperventilating. Nobody was in doubt that my wolf was on board, this was just how things went when you were officially mating.

Not that I was complaining. Ricky's wolf made sure to check very thoroughly.

Ricky took his time making his way back up, enjoying what he had bypassed before. His lips did eventually make it back to mine, where they stayed for another moment. I whimpered as he moved away.

He couldn't get his voice to work so he made a rolling gesture with his hand.

My wolf hummed as she followed his command, rolling us over, onto our knees. When it came to mating, the first part had to be done in a more traditional wolf way. I could feel Ricky's rough hands rubbing along my sides, moving up. With one hand on my shoulder, he went where no male, wolf or human, had ever been.

My head snapped back, as we let out a scream.

Ricky soothingly rubbed his hand up and down my back, giving my body time to adjust, then continued. Soon, my screams were no longer ones of pain.

When his hand began shifting to a paw, he softly, yet forcefully, rotated me onto my side. I could feel certain other parts enlarging as well. It was surprisingly not unpleasant.

When I could feel what we called the knot, I slowly rolled to my back. Ricky immediately went to my neck, kissing it, licking it, devouring it. At the same moment I felt his teeth getting longer, mine did as well.

In perfect synchronization, the way only true soul mates could do, we bit into the other's neck, right above the collar bone. That was also the moment Ricky's wolf released his markings.

Feeling sated and complete, our wolves retreated to the back of our minds. Ricky looked down into my natural light blue eyes and grinned.

Mine.

I giggled as his one word thought swam into my head. *Yours.*

I yelped as his mouth attacked mine again. I had heard many times how overwhelming it could be after a mating. The onslaught of thoughts and feelings, from both of you, could be difficult to handle.

Feeling Ricky's immense love for me was like an aphrodisiac. I couldn't get enough of him. Nor him me. The only thoughts that were discernible were the *I love yous*, which were frequent.

We spent the night under the stars. Loving each other, sleeping, and loving each other again.

CHAPTER 25

Eric

I sucked in a breath when Cassie came through that door, looking like an Amazon princess coming to punish the wicked males. My wolf and I had already come to the decision to back off when Cassie and Ricky got their second chance.

Seeing as how my brother was a shell of a male, and I, while still sad, was also still functioning. I knew who needed her the most.

I had thought about telling him to go find her, to give him my permission to claim his mate, so many times since I graduated. Unfortunately, I was a giant chicken and never opened my mouth. Now, I was going to have to man up and do it.

I braced myself to do so, without even needing to consult my wolf first, right as another scent hit me. One that called to me on a more primal level. My eyes met the greenest set I had ever seen before. They belonged to the blonde goddess standing behind Cassie.

The overwhelming sensation of just her scent nearly had me on my knees. Neither of us moved, neither of us looked away. I realized then how wrong I had been about so many things.

Ricky was right, fate knew better than we did.

I was so focused on her that I didn't even notice when Ricky walked away and joined Cassie in the fighting ring. I looked away from the captivating female long enough to see Cassie's wary eyes.

With this new perspective, I felt all the guilt I had been suppressing. Ignoring. The guilt from keeping my brother from what was rightfully his. I didn't even know my mate's name, what she sounded like, anything. Only her scent and her eyes. Yet, I was already missing her presence.

What would it be like days and weeks from now?

I grimaced as Cassie kicked Ricky in the gut with both feet. Now seemed like a good time to tell him. He needed to know that he was fighting for keeps this time.

You really going to let your mate beat you like this? In front of all these males?

Really, Eric? Now's the time you chose to talk to me? When I am in the middle of a fight?

Yes. You won't let me talk to you any other time.

I laughed as he scowled at me.

Make it quick then. Was he cranky with me for interrupting or the fact that he was getting beat by a female?

I just have one thing that needs to be said right now… claim what's yours, little brother.

Ricky froze. Probably shocked. That seemed to be enough for Cassie to realize someone was talking to him. Her eyes snapped to mine, and she looked… apprehensive. Yes, I was right to do this.

Thank you, brother.

My eyes flicked back to my green-eyed beauty, who was studying me and Ricky both. Her eyes widened, and her mouth made a small "o" shape. Then she started laughing. I watched as she whispered something to the female next to her.

Now they were both looking at me. It felt uncomfortable. The other female had a darker shade of blonde hair, a smidge taller, and features that were more hardened.

I glanced up once more, checking on the two fighting, just in time to see my brother take a very painful hit.

Is that really the best you can do, little brother?

Shut up. He replied in a groan.

I chuckled and turned to the male my brother had been talking to when I came in. It suddenly dawned on me that he must be Cassie's brother Pat. Which would explain the scowl he had given me when I came in.

"Who is the female with the light blonde hair?"

He gave me a wary look before answering. My father was watching Ricky but listening to us.

"That's our cousin Tasha. Why?"

I shook my head. No way I was telling a male I didn't know before I even had a chance to speak to her.

"How much does she know?" I asked him, hoping he would know what I was talking about.

"Everything. Cas has always been close to both of them. That's why I insisted she come here with me. My sister has been walking around like a freaking zombie since she left *him*."

I didn't miss how he left me out of it. It was all because she missed Ricky, her rightful mate.

About then, I heard Cassie mentioning Yolanda.

Sorry, dude. I've been talking to Jordan. Who probably passed the message on.

"I am glad you did. Hopefully, they will have fixed everything by the end of the night."

Pat gave me a confused look. My father on the other hand looked triumphant.

I looked away from Pat again. Tasha was watching, lifting her eyebrows, and licking her lips. She looked like a female preparing to take on a dare. A look that was both a warning and a threat. She was the living embodiment of a "Caution: handle with care. Contents will burn you," label.

I liked playing with fire. I liked taking risks and seeing how far I could push things. I folded my arms across my chest and held my balance. I shot her a wink as I grinned. A "try me" look.

Even from across the gym floor, I could see the heat in her eyes.

They flashed quickly to the side exit, then back to me. She whispered something to her sister again, and then took off.

"If you'll excuse me gentlemen. I have a fated mate to catch." I stepped behind them and quietly chased after her. I heard the ghost of my father's chuckle following behind me.

I made it about fifteen feet out the door before I was knocked onto the ground and pinned.

"So. You're Eric, huh?" Her voice was like a bird singing.

I chuckled. "And you're Tasha. Beautiful name for a beautiful female."

She threw her head back and laughed joyfully. My wolf was panting at the sight of her long slender neck.

"Your sweet little lines aren't going to work on me. I already know everything about you. Insider information and all." Her face fell and she grew melancholy. Probably remembering why she knew all those things. "Are you still in love with my cousin? Cause, that's not going to fly with me."

I shook my head. "No. Cassie is a gem, and she would have been a good mate, but she was never meant to be mine. I'd like to say that I would have handled things better had they just been honest and told me. But I have a feeling we both know that would be a lie. My pride was hurt. I do care about Cassie. She meant a lot to me. I can promise you this though, Tasha, you will always be the only female in my heart."

"I better be. We both know I can kick your arse from here until Sunday, and don't think I won't do it either." She shifted her weight over me, placing herself in a spot that was far from uncomfortable. Her eyes twinkled.

She knows how to play. My wolf was thrilled with the idea.

That had always been his only hang-up with Cassie, she was too innocent. We had hoped that would change after the mating. My father was right, I had been trying to mold her into something she wasn't.

She wasn't Tasha.

I couldn't not retaliate. I lifted my hips enough to brush against her. She was wearing these very short shorts, similar to the ones Cassie slept in. The ones she had been wearing when we showed up early to take her home with us.

Tasha hissed and her eyes rolled to the back of her head. I may not be as good of a fighter as Ricky, but I knew enough. I used that moment of distraction and rolled us over. I even managed to keep our waists right where they were.

Tasha hummed as her fingernail lightly scratched from the side of my forehead, down my cheek, jaw, and neck. When it reached my shirt, she gripped the collar in her hands, and pulled me down. As soon as my lips were on hers, her legs came up and wrapped around my thighs.

I was in heaven. And then I was on my back again. My wolf didn't care that she kept getting the upper hand. Just the opposite, he was thrilled.

Tasha pulled away laughing. I pinched her side, making her squeal. We both jumped when we heard the glass doors in the front of the gym slam against the wall. Cassie ran by, not even seeing us, seconds later.

Tasha jumped to follow, trying to call after her. I swiftly followed her and grabbed her wrist, pulling her back.

"Stay."

She swung an irritated look my way.

Fix it, fix it! My wolf was panicking, probably afraid to lose another mate.

Shut up, I will.

"Sorry, I'm not trying to boss you. Just… wait. Please."

"Why? Cassie needs me." I could hear how much she loved Cas and wanted to help, so I pulled her against my chest. My wolf and I both wanted to comfort her.

"You're not the one who needs to do it. She needs her mate. Trust me. I know my brother. Ten more seconds, tops."

Tasha turned, just in time to see Ricky come flying after Cas, seven seconds later. Tasha sighed and relaxed into my arms.

A moment later, Lauren came hurrying out the side door, a male I hadn't met yet, following on her heels.

"Which way did she go?"

Tasha pointed towards a batch of trees. "That way. Ricky went with her though."

Lauren shook her head. "I'm not sure she wants him to." Lauren started walking fast in the direction they went.

Soon, all three of them were running. I caught up to them quickly. I ran in front of them and cut them off. Raising my arms in the air.

"Leave them be. They need to settle this on their own."

"Why? So, you can feel better?" Lauren snapped.

Tasha hissed at her sister in my defense.

"No. Because they have had enough interference from everyone else. They've never had a chance to just be them. They need a chance to build a real relationship together."

I sniffed the air, realizing there was a strong concentration of both their scents nearby. I took a few steps to the side and found a pile of both their clothes. I laughed.

"They both shifted, which means they are going to have to talk it out… in the buff." I looked at Lauren. "How well can you fight with your mate when neither of you are dressed?" I was assuming that was who he was anyway. Judging by the look they shared and the blush, I was right.

"Alright, but if they don't come back soon, I'm going on a hunt."

I pressed my lips together. "At least give them until morning. They've both been miserable for months."

Tasha laughed then stood on her toes and kissed my cheek. I hadn't realized how tiny she actually was until that moment. I had always dated females who were average height to tall. Tasha was nearly a foot shorter than me.

Her attitude makes her seem taller. I like it.

"Now that that has been settled. Let's go eat, I'm starving."

Tasha pouted at Lauren's words. "Wait! We never got to serve our own slices of humble pie! I like beating up on the males."

I pulled her into my waist and bent down to her ear. "Sweetheart, you can beat me up as often as you want."

She giggled, seeming happy with that compromise. She took my hand and practically dragged me along with them. And, for the first time, I didn't mind someone else being in control.

CHAPTER 26

Ricky

I woke up the next morning, content and confused. Why was I sleeping naked in the middle of this horrid desert? I had hardly slept at all since we got here. It was too freaking hot! Why would I be asleep outside, without an air conditioner?

I heard a yawn and felt someone stirring from behind me. Then I felt two delicate hands wrapping around my waist. I chuckled as I realized that the best dream I had ever had, was in fact reality.

I carefully rolled over, spying my beautiful mate, covered in dirt and her hair all a mess.

Good morning, beautiful.

She sighed and pushed herself into my arms more, laying her head on my forearm. *Good morning.* Her deep sigh of contentment was an amazing boost to my pride.

Are you ready to go back yet? Our families are probably worried.

No, not yet. I bet I look ridiculous.

I smiled and kissed the top of her dirty head. *You look more beautiful than I've ever seen you.*

She gave me an adorable playful scowl, which had me kissing her again. We didn't stop until we reenacted what got us both so dirty in the first place.

Once we had thoroughly greeted the morning, in the best way possible, we took advantage of the spring nearby. It wasn't exactly deep enough to bathe in, but it would work in a pinch.

I helped my mate rinse out her hair, as well as the rest of her. I was ready to get her dirty again, but my father had the worst timing ever.

I hope you are both safe somewhere.

Yes, father. We spent the night nearby. We needed time to talk.

And hopefully end this mess. He grunted. *Does Allen have a replacement Gamma?*

I chuckled, drawing Cassie's attention.

"My father." I explained and she nodded her head.

Yes, father. I will be taking over as Gamma, just as planned. Now we just have to find a Luna.

He snorted, a sound I didn't hear often from him. *That won't be a problem. It seems your mate's cousin was fated for him.*

I nearly fell over laughing. Fate had the worst sense of humor in the world.

While I am happy for you, pup. We still have work that needs to be done here.

Yes, father. We are cleaning up in a spring now and will head back soon.

Good. Meet me back in our cabin, bring my daughter-in-law with you. I want to see her too.

I cut him off and turned to Cassie, who was sitting in the water, waiting, with her hands floating on the top of the small ripples. I sat next to her and laced my right hand with her left.

"Time to go?" Her voice was soft and sweet.

"Yes, I came here on pack business. It still needs to be attended to." I swallowed, knowing I needed to ask this next part, but afraid too. "Will you be coming home with me? I will take over as Gamma in a month. I can't leave my pack yet. If you don't want to come permanently, just give me time and I will find a replacement. I will go wherever you are. I can't bear losing you again."

Cassie laid her head on my shoulder. "I know what you said about Eric last night, but I'm still worried. Will it hurt him to see us together every day?"

I laughed softly. "No. That will no longer be a problem. One of your cousins graciously took care of that for us."

Her head shot up and she looked at me with shock and worry. "Which one? What did she do? Did she hurt him? They both wanted a turn to kick his butt after everything that happened."

I chuckled and leaned in to kiss her lips softly. "No. Turns out, one of your cousins is Eric's fated mate."

Cassie's eyes widened. Then she nearly fell over laughing. I waited until she was wiping the tears from under eyes.

She took a few breaths before explaining. "Sorry. Tasha, the only one who wasn't already mated, is a handful. She's stubborn as a mule. She's also crazy, energetic, has a sassy mouth, a giant heart, and every bit the whore he was. She will definitely keep him in line." She sighed happily and stood up, lowering her hand down for me.

"Let's go home, Ricky."

My wolf and I howled with happiness as we jumped up to join her. We did it a little too fast and started to slip on the moss below us. Cassie laughed with glee as she steadied us.

"I can't wait for you to see the cottage I bought for you."

She froze, making me worry I did something wrong. Then turned with a blush and small smile.

"You bought me a house? But you didn't know if I was coming back."

I shrugged, trying to feign nonchalance. "I hoped. Just because I hadn't come yet, doesn't mean I never would have." I closed the distance between us and placed my palm on her cheek. "You were always meant to be mine, Cassie. I love you."

She tipped herself up on her toes and kissed me softly. "I love you, too. I can't wait to see the home you got us."

We shifted and ran back to where we left our clothes. I half expected Eric to have taken them and hidden them. If it hadn't been for him being distracted by his own mate, he probably would have.

Once dressed, I led Cassie to one of the visitor cabins near the pack house. Since there were so many of us on this trip, Alpha Roger let us stay there. We walked into the cabin and were met by my pack members, as well as Tasha and Pat. Who were all waiting semi-anxiously for us to return.

Tasha ran and pounced on Cassie first. Both of them giggling. She was tiny, even compared to Cas. Eric was right behind her. He apologized to both of us and gave us both hugs. I lifted an eyebrow at his odd behavior. He just shrugged and pulled Tasha back into his arms.

Pat came next. I could tell Cassie was saying something to him in his head. She was scowling, he was grinning. Then she stuck out her tongue at him and he started laughing. He then kissed her cheek and gave her a hug.

Allen was next, patting me on the shoulder and giving my mate a hug. "I'm happy to finally meet you, Cassie. I must say, I enjoyed watching you take this male down a few notches yesterday. Maybe you two can work something out to train a few females in our pack. I can think of a few that would enjoy it."

Cassie beamed at him. "I would love to!" I wrapped my arm back around her waist, squeezing her to me.

My father was the last one to greet us. He gave her a big hug and held her tight. "I told you everything would work out." He stepped back and looked at both of us, then my brother and his mate. "When Roger told me about his new doctor, I had hoped that Cassie would come down with him. This has worked out much better than even I expected. Fate may go about things in an odd way, confusing to us, painful to us, but it always has a purpose. As long as you don't give up, it all straightens out in the end."

He clapped his hands together, then rubbed them. "Now, we males have business to attend to. You females need to start packing. We leave in two days. Then we have one month before leadership transfers over to the next generation." He leaned down and gently kissed them both on the cheeks. "Welcome to the family, both of you."

Eric and I both kissed our mates goodbye and followed him and Allen out.

CHAPTER 27

Cassie

We waited until they were far enough away, then Tasha and I squealed, laughed, and then hugged again.

"I can't believe you are Eric's fated mate." I sniffed the air and gasped. "And you already did the deed?"

She shrugged, failing at putting up the not caring front. "Why wait? Besides, like Charles said, we only have a matter of days until we need to leave."

I took her hand and dragged her toward the door. "We are going to head back to your house, and you are going to explain everything that happened last night...well almost everything." Tasha laughed. She was the queen of TMI.

"You females have fun with that. I have to get to the hospital." Pat gave me one more hug, then Tasha. "Congratulations to both of you. I'm truly happy for you. I'm glad that you will be together. I won't worry as much."

I snorted. Yeah, right.

Pat walked down the path a different way than us. As soon as he was gone, Tasha started telling me what happened.

"Girl! I can't tell you how funny it was when I realized who he was. I told Lauren of course, and we were both busting up. I had such a hard time focusing on your fight, but I knew we needed to get a few things straight first. So, I had him follow me out."

I wrapped an arm around her shoulders as we walked. "I am so happy for you two. I nearly fell over laughing when I heard, but still. I do think you two will be perfect together. If anyone can reign the other one in, it will be you two. All though, with you two together, I can imagine some serious damage being done."

We both laughed and joked all the way back to Uncle Cameron's house. I had chosen to stay with them when we arrived. I wanted my brother and his new mate to have some privacy.

Lauren and their mother were waiting for us, with breakfast. Which I happily ate before taking a real shower. My poor mate hadn't even had time to change clothes before he headed out to work.

All four of us spent the day packing. Most of my stuff was still back home in Alaska. Later that night, Ricky and I worked out our schedule. Once the conference was over, he would travel home with me for a week.

It was a great week at that. My parents, as well as my Alpha and Luna (who insisted on seeing that I was truly happy finally), loved him. We shipped all but a couple bags worth of clothes to my new pack, those flew home with us.

Luna Bea balled as she hugged me. I wasn't sure who was happier that I was there. Bea or Ricky.

I fell in love with our little cottage the moment I saw it. It was perfect for us. There were three bedrooms inside, and two bathrooms. We had so much space on the outside that we could build on if we wanted too.

A few weeks later, the pack leadership transferred over. The whole pack was relieved that the Alpha role was able to be handed down. Most of them had been worried. It was rare that the eldest son would not be able to take up the mantle, let alone either of the sons.

The first year was amazing. Ricky was the best mate anyone could ask for. He would also make the best father of our unborn pup. Tasha and I both found out we were pregnant together. We planned on telling them together too.

Tasha had a degree in childhood education, so she worked part-time in the shifter-only daycare on the pack grounds. I decided to be a nurse, something Ricky fully supported.

Ricky and Eric were back to being the best of friends, Travis right along with them. Mary, Travis' mate, who was wonderfully awesome, was the one who suggested we both might be pregnant. Our three families were as close as could be.

Charles and Bea moved into a cabin of their own, insisting that Eric and Tasha have full run of the pack house. Really, I think they wanted to take full advantage of their retirement. Who could blame them after thirty years of running this pack, and the town?

With the help of Dr. Shapiro, we figured out the day our smells would be changing, announcing to the world that we had pups growing inside us. We were only a few days apart. Tasha and I told our mates we were going to visit our family in California for a few days, they grumbled and whined.

We spent a lovely few days there. Thankfully it was fall, and at least a few degrees cooler. Mary picked us up a day earlier than the official plans, not letting our mates know we were back in town. We stayed hidden with the grandparents-to-be until the pack Halloween party. It coincided perfectly.

Our mates were sitting in the front living room, which was made for just such an occasion. Tasha and I both just walked in. They jumped up as soon as they smelled us, knocking our breaths out when they collided with us.

After the all too brief hugs, they stepped back, sniffing and studying both of us. We laughed at their confused expressions. They looked at each other, mentally talking it out.

"Trying to figure out whose smell changed?" I asked them sardonically, holding back my laughter.

Tasha leaned to me, a hand covering her mouth, as she mock-whispered to me. "For an Alpha and a Gamma, they are mighty slow, aren't they?"

I nodded. "Maybe we should take a few steps away from each other."

"We probably should, they look like they could use a little help."

Our audience laughed, our mates did not.

At least they weren't until we moved away from the other couple. They both grinned, howled and lifted us up, spinning us. Their howls were echoed around the room and outside by the rest of the pack.

The party turned into a celebration. We had come up with many different ways to surprise them, but we settled on simplicity, and teasing them.

At one time in my life, I wasn't sure what I wanted. A fated mate or a chosen one? I still didn't understand why things took the route they did. There was still a good chance of us meeting eventually, thanks to the regional conferences.

There were times I wondered what if I had mated with Eric in college, before meeting his parents. I had no doubts that we would have been happy, but not at peace. Not the kind of peace that our fated mates gave us.

I had nothing against those who chose their mates, after all, Pat and Stacey were a great example of choosing it right. But there was nothing I would trade my fated mate for.

For being such a twisted witch, Fate sure knew what she was doing. There was no better mate for Eric than Tasha. And there was no better mate for me than Ricky.

He was truly the missing piece to my soul.

THE WEIRD WORLD OF TJ LEE

The Cooper Family Chronicles
- Love, Devotion, and Trust...with a side of Brownies (Levi & Callie)
- For Ellie (Emma & Freddie)
- For Emma (Emma & Freddie Cont./Rick & Rachel)
- Forgive & Forget (Tim & Alicia/Zack & Zoey)
- Avenging Angel (Mitch & Charity)

Dark Protectors (frequent crossovers with the Coopers)
- Daughter For Sale (Eli & Vanessa)
- Heartbeats (Alyssa & Ryan)
- Sins of the Mother (Trixie & Ty)

Million Dollar Duet (Crossovers with the Coopers)
- Million Dollar Angel (Elizabeth & Antonio)
- Million Dollar Screw Up (Stacey & Ricky)

Standalone novels (still have crossovers with the others)
- Finding My Sunrise (Samantha/Sarah & Jackson)
- 2 Doors Down (Rose & Ryan)
- Last Christmas (Trish & Noah)

The Yin & Yang Collection (you guessed it, slight crossover here too)
- Oil & Water (Mia & Theo)
- Scalpels & Staples (Sheila & Jeremiah)

The Silver Moon Collection
- Ivory Snow (Snow White - Shifter Style)
- Now Until Forever (Jessica & Jake)
- Fate Vs Choice (Cassie & Ricky)

The Cursed Ones
- Revolution
- The Birth of a Queen
- The Witch's Curse

ABOUT THE AUTHOR

TJ is an avid reader. Reading was always an escape for her in her crazy messed up world. She's always had a vivid imagination. It wasn't until she was locked in her house for a year and a half, with only her two young kids, and two dogs to talk to, that she finally started writing. She found an even better escape.

TJ is a High School English teacher and a single mom. She holds a Bachelor's degree in Cultural Anthropology and Master's in Cultural Responsive Education. Her life motto, one she says with her students regularly, is to "fly your weird flag high!" She wants everyone to learn to be true to who they are. Accept yourself the way you are. Love yourself the way you are.